I0822280

Hermosa, A Novel

Hermosa, A Novel

Peter Slavin

Pete Slavin
Hermosa, A Novel

Published by
Lilliworks Active Learning Foundation

First Edition, 2025

Cover Design by Pete Slavin
PO Box 6426
Moraga, CA 94570
(510) 814-9111
Peteslavin.com

ISBN: 979-8-9912417-6-2
Library of Congress pending
Printed in USA

FOR CRICKET AND PICKLE

1

Last thing done for today. After a thorough inspection of the Porter Ranch property, James anticipated his upcoming project, which involved constructing a few new residences on a small, predominantly level piece of land.

The property was sold at auction last month for $1.4m. On it stood one tired, 1950's era four bedroom, four bath California Ranch style house on 3.2 acres. It was built inside a secluded canyon behind some orange groves in the hills above the San Fernando Valley by the owner of a medium-sized orchard. Franklin Thomas, the orchard owner, selected a popular builder and went for the standards of the time, with big windows set behind low eaves to keep the heat down. Built-in pool. Wet bar. It was all very modern for 1953.

As the population grew and people moved out to the suburbs of Los Angeles, the orange groves were sold off to big developers, bringing in a good sum of money to the aging rancher and his wife, which they left to their son Reginald. Throughout the '80s, Reggie squandered as much as he could in as short a period of time as possible, venturing into terrible film making endeavors and developing an extra-large penchant for cocaine and adult film stars.

With his films not doing well, Reggie Thomas attempted to diversify and started a project to develop the small canyon that enclosed his parents' property. He could simply mimic the developers that were building out the orange groves around him, which couldn't be difficult. He brought in a Project Manager and set him to work, not knowing how much the infrastructure would cost. By 1991 he was completely out of money.

The house changed hands a few times after Reggie left, became a rental for six years, never getting far from a state of disrepair, and was finally sold at auction. It's only redeeming value for James was that Reggie's PM had completed most of the groundwork for six new houses to be built in the small canyon and the one to be rebuilt. Now, premier houses in the area went for somewhere in the $2.5m range.

-

James was driving down out of the hills, downshifting Grandpa's orange 1968 Dodge Power Wagon with windows cranked down and the radio on low. It was a beautiful March afternoon in the Valley. In jeans, his favorite t-shirt and his comfy Asics, James knew there would only be a few nice days of spring in this particular area before the temperature climbed up into the high '90s and he was soaking it in. The hills were still mostly green, on their way to brown soon. Barely a whisper of a breeze.

It would be a little better if he had plans for Friday night but, what can you do. He'll get up early and get stuff done on Saturday morning. He just spent $1.4 million of company money on the property and should get started on it.

-

Lauren changed out of her work clothes and into the sundress that was hanging in her locker for the last few weeks. The weather has been cool and damp (it doesn't really rain in Southern California and it's never *cold* cold) so she hadn't changed out of her work clothes before leaving in a while. She parked in the hospital overflow lot a few blocks south from the doctor lot because liked the short walk to her car after work, in her head separating herself from the office, even though she loved her job and had to walk along the noisy overpass of the 118 freeway.

The security guard offered to give her a ride but she declined, citing the beautiful weather, but in fact he had given her *that* look several times, and she didn't want to encourage him. The weather was beautiful, and he was nice enough, and cute, probably harmless, but most certainly not her type. Her type was as yet undefined, but it was definitely not married guys fifteen years her senior.

As she was thinking about her type, movement on her left came into her periphery, very close. She jump-turned to see a white van coming to a stop at the curb near her and a muscly giant in a painted-on black t-shirt and jeans step out of the sliding door before the van even came to a full stop. What the hell?

-

As he was coasting up to the red light at Rinaldi St., James spotted a girl walking along the sidewalk on right side of the street in a black-and-yellow flowered sundress. He later said he noticed her because no one walks in LA, especially not in the North Valley, but in truth it was more about the long dark brown hair, the way the sundress moved, the Converse hi-tops.

He wasn't thinking anything dirty; It was like watching moving art to James. After all, the female form is arguably the most popular subject of art in history.

While he was watching, he saw a white Ford van pull up next to her and a middle linebacker step out. She turned suddenly to her left to face the huge person that stepped out of the van and attempted to back away...

-

The monster grabs Lauren's upper left arm, hard, and starts to pull her toward the open door. He was well over 6', impossibly strong and wearing an ugly expression on his face. Dark hair, square jaw. She attempted to yell but couldn't catch her breath (maybe panic?) but probably wouldn't be heard over the ocean-like sounds of the 118 freeway below them anyway. It comes out more as an, 'Aye Aye', like she was trying to explain herself. She thinks, 'he has the wrong person', for no reason she could think of. Square head turns to his right for a split second as he is backing into the van, still with her upper left arm painfully clamped when the van disappeared with a boom and was replaced by an old orange truck.

-

James, rolling downhill through the now-green light, shifted into 3rd and stepped on the gas to pick up speed. There is no other traffic or any parked cars on this street, even though he has just passed the hospital on his left. He's crossing on the overpass of the 118 freeway and traffic below is moving in both directions, odd for this time of day. The massive guy attempting to drag the girl hears him at the last minute. The driver looks in the rear view. James hit the back driver's side of the van in the neighborhood of forty-five miles an hour. This is absolutely devastating to the van, getting hit by a truck made with steel I beams as a chassis, and worse for the slab of human in the sliding doorway. As the van shoots forward, the right side hops up onto the sidewalk and it smashes into a light pole.

-

Lauren almost loses her balance when her arm is released, since she was pulling away from square head with all that her small frame could muster. She stumbles, collects herself under her Chuck Taylors, and starts to run back the way she came. Where did that orange truck come from? She must have been distracted by the monster trying to take her into the obligatory *white van...*

-

James' first thought was that the Power Wagon stalled but no, it was still running. It just couldn't be heard after the tremendous sound of the collision that was still ringing in his ears and freeway noise below. Thankfully there are no deployed airbags to have to work around. At that moment, he is grateful for the massive steel truck. He also gets the major urge to get out of there before the van people see him, thinking that there must be some omnipresent, movie bad guy who has access to street cameras and credit cards. He looked to his right but the girl is gone. How long had he been thinking all of this? A second? Was he concussed?

-

Lauren runs back toward the hospital, looking over her shoulder, back at the van. She gets a terrible feeling that the kidnappers are not really injured but about to spring out of the van and run after her. She knows this is wrong but can't calm herself enough to slow down and keeps running.

-

With a slight grinding of the big stick shift, James reverses to catch up to the girl in the sundress and yells, 'Hop in'. He tried to be somewhat casual, possibly even comforting, but it came out weird to his ears, like as if he does this all the time. Great.

-

She hears the orange pickup driver and stops, looking back again at the van and notes that feeling that they are coming for her is still there. She feels like she has been running for a while but it had only been three seconds and she is almost in the same place. She makes a mental note of this for her research on panic. She looks at the pickup driver, sees the honest look on his face and makes the decision to get in, needing to be far away, needing to be in a car or a truck that will get her out of here *now*. The Converse were not cutting it.

-

James leaned over to pull up the door lock for her, thinking that she might not think of that. She gets in the truck and slams the door hard and he swings a U-turn heading up Porter Ranch Road, where he came from. Lauren fumbles around for the shoulder seat belt but this thing doesn't have one, only a lap belt. She gives up quickly on the seat belt for now. James' focus at this point is everywhere but intense at the same time. He sees the road ahead, the van in his rear view not moving, the two oncoming cars on the cross street he is coming up to, the engine temperature gauge. He can operate that way. He thinks he lost the grille of Grampa's pickup but doesn't know for sure. It has the original black license plate and only one on the back so he couldn't have lost a front plate. There is a small hiss coming from the front of the truck. Radiator? Probably a hose, and he knows with certainty that they will have to park it somewhere before it dies on them.

He thinks, how many orange 1968 Dodge Power Wagons were registered in the area? Probably not many. Someone could find out through the DMV, if that is really a thing and not just a movie thing, which he thinks it might be. But who was chasing him? Wait, them. He suddenly realized that the girl in the sundress was on the other side of the bench seat from him and had spoken, looking at him wide-eyed.

-

'Why would you do that?', she had said. He still might be concussed, even though he is pretty positive that he didn't hit the steering wheel or the windshield. 'Were they trying to kidnap you?', James replies, 'Are you okay? Who could just drive past a kidnapping? And how is that your first question?'. Lauren confirms she's okay and introduces herself as Lauren. James says James.

-

She says, 'You don't look hurt, Jimmy. Are you okay?' and leans over the bench seat to look at him a little closer. He nods and she picks up on his discomfort but not sure which he is visibly uncomfortable with, her closeness, pain or the familial use of his name. Probably the latter, since he introduced himself as 'James' and not 'Jimmy'.

She thinks he looks too intense, like he is going to have a stroke, and says, 'Is this how you normally pick up girls?'. She smiles, still looking him over for injuries or blood patches, hoping to lighten the situation just a little. It works and he smiled a slight smile that touched his eyes.

'Is it that obvious?', James replies, looking serious for a second before the corner of his mouth ticks up a touch.

As she sits back in her part of the wide truck cab, she thinks, this guy is nice enough to risk his life for her, which is *weird*. Her friends wouldn't help her move, no less risk life and limb for her or anyone else. In general, LA is a selfish sort of place. Her smile doesn't last long because the experience of what just happened jumps back into the foreground.

| 7 | –

There is no damage to the windshield so he (probably) hadn't hit his head, but she wasn't sure his head could get to the windshield with that giant steering wheel in the way. He's wincing though and she thinks that he might have some sort of impact trauma. Wrists, shoulders, maybe ribs on the steering wheel since there is no airbag. Whiplash? Should be but he looks strong so maybe not. She puts on the lap belt.

Lauren has always had a keen understanding of her immediate situation, able to get a fast read on people and her surroundings. The topic of this had always interested her greatly and she was building her career around it. She was currently a resident neuroscientist at Mission Hills hospital in Granada Hills, with her focus being on cognitive psychology.

She could see his face when he hit the van, in that split second, and that he didn't look horrified. He looked determined. He had a certain Mark Whalberg look about him, wide-eyed and cute in a very American way. Gym body but not bulky like the square headed guy. Clean cut. The whites of his eyes so white that he obviously hadn't had a drug near his system since his mom's epidural. He could be twenty-three, could be thirty-three. Jeans, STP t-shirt (band or motor oil?) and old running shoes. No lines or wrinkles around his periwinkle blue eyes or grays in his short, sandy brown hair that looks *shaped,* which looks expensive. Periwinkle, she thinks, is something she may have never actually thought before.

He watches the road and his rear-view mirrors intensely, always looking for threats, eyes moving. And was that lavender she smelled in this old truck? It should smell like a combination of rust, mold and sweat, Lauren thinks.

-

James had grown up in LA proper, Mid-Wilshire in fact, from his birth to sophomore year of high school before his little family moved up to the San Fernando Valley. They had moved out of the four-plex and into the 'big house' in 2013. James played football at his new school and was very good but didn't make long lasting friendships there or a career of it at 5'10". His football friends were still around, and he hung out with them on occasion, but were more like acquaintances than real friends. He didn't stay in close contact with his two real LA friends, still playing online games on occasion with the nerdy one, the other seeming to be surviving off of social drugs and EDM shows, according to his Instagram.

When he was younger, he assumed that he and his high school girlfriend, Becca, would meet up again after college and get married. They had been through a lot together. They started dating at 15. He was there for her when her parents fought and she had been there for him when his parents had died in a car accident when he was 17. They had gone off to separate colleges at 18 and he went to visit at his first opportunity, only to find her naked with a guy in her dorm. He thought he could overlook that after school since they said they weren't going to be *exactly* exclusive, but he found out through a friend that she had slept with someone else *before* leaving for college.

So, James was alone a lot.

-

'We should get somewhere safe to think about this', James says. 'I know a place. First though we need to switch out this truck.'

'Ok' Lauren says, a little disconnected as she thinks, who has extra cars? They can't be very nice if this old truck is his first choice.

Through a short and not-uncomfortable silence, he turns left, right and right again and in just a few minutes they are in the driveway of a white-and-brown, single-story house. It appears to be older, built in the '60s or '70s, looking very Brady Bunch. He pulls a garage door remote out from a cubby in the dashboard, points it at the three-car garage and hits a button. The double door rolls up and a single door stays down. He rolls the truck towards an empty spot as she thinks, it's too tall for the garage and, do I want to be inside a closed garage with a total stranger? at the same time but it fits and she goes with it. The inside of the garage is lined with cabinets and is extremely neat. She hops out as soon as he stops.

In the single bay sits an older, black Mercedes-Benz station wagon. It is in very good shape but has a musty feel to it. He pushes a button on the wall and the single door opens all the way before he pushes another button to close the double door. She knows he did that for her benefit and thinks, he's making me feel comfortable...

When they get out of the truck, they both need to walk around to get in their respective sides of the Mercedes. Lauren looks for James as he walks around the back of the pickup, looking at his face for any malintent there. What she sees is his soft eyes and kind face, and then notices that he is in great shape. Shoe hopes she wasn't noticed when she looked at his arms, chest and shoulders.

Without speaking, they get into the Mercedes, buckle up and back out. He pushes a button on the visor and the single garage door rolls down. On a smaller street but moving again, Lauren says, 'When did your parents pass away?' James visibly starts when she says it and after a brief pause says, 'Oh no, this isn't going to work long term if you are going to be that perceptive.'

'Long term? We just met fifteen minutes ago.' Lauren has her lips parted as she feigns incredulity, but the corners of her mouth are turned up slightly. She has always liked seeing people's first reaction to her perception, which was usually more disbelief than this. He is accepting but was also able to make it funny quickly. He's sharp.

'That may be true but I will *never* be able to make an entrance like *that* again so this has to work.', James says through the upturned corners of his mouth. He made a left turn on a two lane avenue. 'No pressure', he adds late.

'Ok, where are you taking me? Someplace public? I don't think you're a weirdo, because if you are, you would have wanted to stay in that clean garage.' Lauren replies. 'Maybe some zip ties, a little duct tape. Very Dexter in there.'

'You already know I'm not a weirdo. Someone as smart as you figured that out already. But no, not someplace public until we can figure out what that was all about and what to do next.'

He risked a look over at her as he was looking for oncoming traffic to the right. Her hair was dark brown and her face shape was somewhat oval with high cheekbones, almond-ish eyes, a little mixed-race exotic. Light brown skin. He liked it.

Lauren noticed the look but didn't mention it. 'Mmm. Okay but I get to approve the place.', she says. Then, a long pause and one side of her mouth turns up in a half-smile. 'Weirdo.'

He smiled a little at her comment and says, 'How did you know about my parents? I was very impressed but was trying not to show it. I didn't want to feed some massive, brain-surgeon-style ego you might have.'

'I studied the brain and behavioral science in school.' Lauren said. 'You didn't say we were swinging by *your* house to get another car, you just said we were getting another car. And when we got there, you didn't go inside to let anyone know we were there. The air was a little stale and everything clean but felt dusty and unused. The inside looked a little dated. You're not wearing a ring so most likely no wife and kids in that family house. The ten-year-old Mercedes with very little mileage on it.'

'So you're a brain surgeon! That is definitely not going to help me look good here.' James said, slightly animated, leaning forward toward the steering wheel a little, teasing. 'But yeah, nine years ago, car accident.'

'I'm sorry to hear that. Must have been tough at that age...'

'It was. Wait, you don't know how old I am, do you?' James asked. 'I actually have one thing you haven't already figured out?'

She sighed. 'I haven't figured that out yet.'

'Aha! I'll never tell!'

'BUT,' she continued, 'this car is about 10 years old and it doesn't look like a young person drove it much so you probably had your own car. So, you were seventeen when they passed and are twenty-six now? That right?'

He drove on. 'I feel violated, like I need to put on a second pair of pants to keep myself safe in the future.'

She laughed out loud against her will. 'There was a plaque on the wall in the garage of a high school football team from 10 years ago... so I cheated on that one.' A smile. 'I'm a neuroscience resident at Mission Hills Hospital, not a surgeon. Where are we going?' Serious now but absent-mindedly massaging her upper left arm.

'Sneaky.' James says, 'I work in real estate and have a house that is waiting to be renovated. It's in a company name and not mine just in case someone can hack the DMV record on the truck.'

'Is it close? I'm going to have a look at you when we get there so see where you are hurt.' Lauren says matter-of-factly.

'I'm okay.' James says. 'I've been hit harder than that.' He made another left turn.

'Says the man trying to look tough. That doesn't impress me, if that is what you are trying to do. I'm not a fan of impact sports. Goes with the career,' said Lauren.

'Oh, I was definitely trying to impress you. I'm going to be overcompensating here for a long time. There are serious inadequacy ramifications to you being that smart and having a job like that.'

'The fragile male ego, right out there on display! That's impressive though, your slightly jovial self-awareness.'

'Jovial? I would have used 'jocular' for that situation.' He said, turning right.

'Jocular?! Holy hell. I think that accident knocked your pocket protector loose,' she said.

'Har har,' James said, but was genuinely smiling. 'Are you hurt? Did I ask earlier?'

'You did but no, not hurt. I might have some arm bruising from where that guy grabbed me but that's probably it.' She looked down at her left arm and then rubbed it again lightly.

'The place we're going to is right up here.' Rear view mirror check. He turned left up a steep road with houses behind a wall on the left and a steep hillside on the right. They climbed in silence for less than a minute as the road curved around to the left. At the top of the climb sat alone a brown house with dark brown wooden shake shingles and a light brown garage door. It was not a very notable house except for the view on the left that looked over the houses that were behind the wall and most of the San Fernando Valley.

'That is a pretty nice view,' Lauren says as they pulled up. She can see clumps of rooftops, an industrial area, a flock?, thicket?, of trees that look like willows on her right.

'It's more impressive at night,' James replied. 'That's why I want to renovate it. It can be much more than it is right now.'

'I was going to make another weirdo comment but I think I want to see it at night,' she says.

'We can sit out front instead of going in. There are some chairs on the patio.'

'No, let's go inside. I'm still a little freaked out.'

He opens a lockbox and retrieves a single key and uses it to open the big, heavy looking (brown, of course) wood front door. He holds the door open and Lauren walks in. The view is at the living room windows and there are a few old but expensive looking mid-century modern pieces of furniture seemingly strewn about randomly on a brown and cream shag rug. The place smells faintly of stale cigarettes and dog, which is what she thought the truck would smell like. A large stone fireplace seemed to grow out of one corner of the room and was taking up large sections of wall on either side.

'There are some waters in the fridge,' James says and heads to the right. Lauren looks out the window at the trees below and at the cemetery on the left, which from here looks like a park. James comes back with 2 bottles of Fiji water.

'You must do well,' Lauren says, accepting the water.

'The house is a company project. I don't actually own it', James says.

'I was referring to the water', she said, and smiled a little. 'Kidding. But a view like this can't be cheap.'

'No, I don't take on cheap projects. I'm lucky enough to be able to select more fun projects.'

'Like?' she questioned. She noticed that he said 'company project' and then said 'he doesn't take on cheap projects'. She assumed, correctly, that he owned the company.

James said, 'Like the little seven house project I just took on in a little canyon in Porter Ranch. I just finished walking through it when I bumped into you.'

Lauren, curious: 'What else?'

James: 'There's a house near Santa Monica that is 90% and a four-plex in LA that is just getting floors.'

In fact, James' company owned thirty-eight houses and fifteen hundred and fifty-six apartments for rent throughout the greater Los Angeles area. His father, a commercial real estate lawyer named Henry, bought his first condo in Mid-Wilshire when he was twenty. He married Jennie, a contract lawyer he met in college, and they expanded. They bought the condo next to them and rented it, eventually buying the rest of the units in the building. Henry did the maintenance and improvements himself, opting to save on upkeep in the early years while still keeping up his full-time job renting commercial properties.

He used the equity from the four-plex and investments from his friends to buy more condos, using contracts drawn up by Jennie, and eventually hiring Jennie's friend Max as his real estate lawyer. His friends were reimbursed well for their contributions and Henry had no problems raising capital from them for more real estate projects.

The company, Mid-Wilshire Investment Group, brought in about $4m per month in revenue. It went to pay back investors, his self-insurance, property taxes, the property management companies that made everything work, etc., but was not his income, despite that fact that Mid-Wilshire Investments was just James now that his parents were gone.

Max was still Mid-Wilshire's lawyer and was like an uncle to him. When his parents passed, Max made sure he went to college, taught him everything he needed to know about the ins-and-outs of the property business, helped manage the money. Max told James that he would never steal from Henry or James because they paid him very well. That was a key concept in business.

His dad taught him that. To take care of the people who take care of you and the renters, who are your customers.

'How did you do during Covid?' Lauren asked.

'I came out even', James states, 'and no one lost their home.' Lauren smiled at that, figuring this guy is nice enough to trash his truck for a stranger, then of course he would make sure no one lost their home. She wasn't sure how long this would last since she could be, different, to use a common word.

'Seems like a strange question but do you know someone who would try to kidnap you? A crazy ex or something?'

'No crazy exes,' she said. Lauren thought for a minute. Her childhood was pretty uneventful, a chubby nerd through middle school and most of high school, staying self-contained except for her best friend. She was a late bloomer for a girl at sixteen, getting taller (she maxed out now at 5'5") and thinner but retaining her chest size. She was a lot more popular in senior year but stayed focused on her studies, making it into UCLA Medical School. No real high school boyfriend, no long term relationships to speak of.

There was the security guard who liked her but she thought he was harmless. There was Dr. McSleazy (her name for him) who seemed like he was trying to fuck everyone in the hospital, possibly even patients. But she figured he didn't really focus on her, just on getting laid. There was the nice guy her friend was always trying to set her up with but she could never remember his name. Lenny? Probably not. She felt bad that she didn't like him even though he was very sweet. Kenny? Damn. She didn't know. Poor Benny.

There was that club owner that hit on her a number of times. She turned from the window and said, 'Chance,' she says finally.

'You think it happened by chance?' James asks.

'No, goofball, there is this guy named Chance.' A crooked half smile from Lauren, 'He owns the Blue Katana night club in Hollywood. He asked me out a few times but I don't think he is used to women rejecting him. He's good looking, has money, dresses well, drives nice cars.' Lauren pauses. 'Do you think we should call the police?"

'That should be first. What? You're looking at me funny.'

'Well Jimmy, I'm worried about that. You drove into a van on purpose, injuring at least one, maybe two people and then fled the scene. You hid the offending vehicle in a garage. I'm pretty sure there are some laws broken there. I didn't see any witnesses to corroborate our story either. Just maybe some upper arm fingerprints which I could have gotten from you.'

'Alright, that's out. I wouldn't be able to protect you if I'm locked up. Maybe we should go to the Blue Banana tonight, pay Chance a visit?'

Lauren thinks, then says, 'Okay we can swing by my place and I can pick up some... okay you're looking at me funny now. What?'

'That's not a good idea. If I was stalking someone, that is the first place I would go.' James states. 'Where is it? The place we're not going to?'

'Sherman Oaks', she says. As they make their way back to the car, Lauren asks, 'What are you thinking?'

James stops to lock the front door and putting the key back in the lockbox.

There was a question of taste. 'Shopping. What is your style? The sun dress doesn't give me any clues. Is it more Melrose-funky or like Nordstrom?', he asked.

'Rodeo, please.' Lauren says in a very bad 'English Butler' style accent. It's terrible. He cringes.

'A brain surgeon that does voice overs. Impressive.' James says with a small smile. 'How about Santa Monica? We can grab some stuff on the way to my place.'

'Where is your place?', Lauren asks.

'Hermosa', he says, meaning Hermosa Beach.

'My turn to be impressed. You have my full attention.' she announces and looks at him face on, standing next to the car.

'It's not big or on the water or anything so don't get your hopes up too much. I did add a small sitting area on the roof to watch the sunset though, which is nice.' He shrugged while he was saying this.

'It could be a doorway and a shopping cart near the beach and I'm all set. You sound like you are apologizing for your house in Hermosa Beach. Weirdo.' Lauren says, grabbing the car door handle. 'Want me to 'Hop In?''

James shook his head. 'Damn. I was hoping you missed that.'

Lauren's family did well. Not Hermosa Beach well but well enough for her to go to medical school and not have to work two jobs. She wasn't super impressed by money but she did like nice things, even if she didn't have a lot of them.

2.

Chance's phone rings. He picks it off the table, slides the green button and says Hello. It's Billy.

'It's me. We didn't make the pickup. Someone rammed us with their truck and almost killed us while we were loading the product.'

'Who would do such a thing?' he asks. 'Are you both okay?'

'I'm fine but Tony's not. He was in the doorway when we were hit. He looked pretty bad.'

'Where is he? And where are you?'

'I dropped him at the hospital and took off. I wiped the van and left it off the street near a body shop, called a cab.'

'Repair shop. That's pretty clever. A damaged van near a shop. And lots of people need a ride from a shop too. Did you call an Uber?'

'No, I used a local cab app. No names.' Billy says.

'Ok good job. How bad is Tony?' Chance asks.

'He's going to be in the hospital a while. He was pretty fucked up.'

'Ah, that sucks. Which hospital? And where do you think she went? Do you think she knew who you guys were?'

Billy thinks. 'She mighta recognized Tony from the club but I doubt it. He's kinda hard to miss but he's not there very much. But no one saw me. She got in the pickup truck that hit us. No idea where she went. Want me to go by her place?'

Chance says, 'No no. Forget the whole thing for now. Text me the name of the hospital and come by the club later.

'Ok will do.' Billy says and hangs up.

-

Christopher William Scott, Billy to his LA acquaintances (he doesn't have friends), is mean. He's always been mean. He grew up in a mean neighborhood with mean kids and mean teachers. Even the weather was mean in his northern Midwest city. He was smaller than most growing up and either lied or made jokes to get out of a lot of fights but got into a million anyway. His parents grew up there and were tougher than the mean kids so (Chris as a child) didn't get sympathy. When he was seventeen years and seven months old, he took some clothes and what money he saved shoveling snow or whatever he stole and left for California where he took up acting.

He was a believable actor, able to channel his childhood experiences for roles but never landed a big role. At 5'8", he was short for California but not for Hollywood. They made that work all the time. He kept himself lean and strong, working out his whole body. He didn't want to get bulky. He hadn't been rock climbing but thought about starting, fearing he might be too old now at thirty-four.

He was tough on people from his upbringing, abrasive actually, but he thought of himself as a realist with no patience for bullshit, down to earth, maybe able to help the airheads here in LA. He had not-exactly standard movie-hero looks with an average thin face, no high cheek bones, no moody brow, no dark eyes. But he did have an agent that knew he could act and that helped him survive on the gigs she got him.

A TV show here, 4th credit in a movie there. And he worked for Chance, who was like him, he thought, but hid it well and had money.

-

Chance Baris moved to the US with his dad when he was a kid. He's pretty sure that his father was a war criminal, fleeing to the US in 1994 during the Bosnian war and changing their name. From what he gathered while the old man was hammered, he thinks he was in charge of Karaman's House, a detention center in Foca that became famous for the rape and mistreatment of women during the war crime tribunal.

His mom Katerina was not a strong person, as he remembers it. Well, that's what his dad always said. She suffered from depression and would stay in bed for days, leaving her only child to fend for himself at a young age. She killed herself when Chance was ten, not making it to the US with him and his dad a year later.

Chance went to school in a not-rich-not-poor section of Burbank, which was major culture shock for him at eleven years old. He didn't fit in at first but figured out how to get around, as kids do. It wasn't very hard for him, since his father taught him that no one was giving anything away in life; you have to take what you wanted. And he did.

Today he spoke almost-unaccented English but struggled with English classes early on. Since language was an issue for him, he took an interest in computers and taught himself how to write a different language, code. At age nineteen, he wrote and patented a greatly improved search engine string of code, which he licensed to Altavista, a web search engine at the time. Altavista was bought by Yahoo!. Yahoo!'s search engine was then merged with Microsoft in 2009 to eventually become Bing. Microsoft still wrote him checks for the code.

He didn't write much computer language after that though, not being able to work for Google out of a conflict of interest and not wanting to move to Seattle for Microsoft. He didn't have to sit in a room by himself anymore, he now had a steady six-figure passive income and can do whatever he wanted. His inner extrovert was waiting to come out. And he wanted to be around women.

He kicked around, not doing much for a few years before he befriended an unsuccessful writer, which was advantageous for Chance. David Whitehall had stories. He had no money and was, for the most part, unemployable as anything but a writer so Chance took him in and gave him a place to stay.

He learned about one of Dave's projects that he thought would sell for sure. A good-looking young couple with no prospects decides to rob stores for money in LA. It had Hollywood all over it and no one likes Hollywood more than Hollywood.

He convinced Dave to put him as a co-author of just that one story so that, in case it sells, the money he would make would repay Chance for everything he had done for him. So Chance took the script and brought it around to some people he knew, who got him to other people and, eventually, the right person. They got an advance and a team to start working on it and Chance got himself a part as the lead's best friend.

Wild and Young did well in theaters but became a cult classic as the start of the careers of the now-movie-star leads. Kate Camilla and Bobby Santiago did the press junkets and 'avoided' questions about their romantic involvement for the tabloids, which helped. And Chance received an Oscar nomination for Best Supporting Actor, mostly for a heavily-directed scene that was done in *only* seventy-eight takes where he begs his best friend not to do the final, and eventually fatal, heist.

The nod gave him notoriety but not acting skills. His next acting gig was a straight-to-DVD flop. He received an Executive Producer credit on Wild though for getting it made, which led him to start his own production company. The projects he worked on now were mostly put together by folks hoping to have their small budget movie turn into a cult classic, like Wild. So far, he hadn't had another one like that but his salary and small percentage usually netted him another mid-six figures. And, as a cult classic, Wild was still funneling money in his direction.

David Whitehall used his portion of the Wild money to move out and try and get one of his other project off the ground, the Fluffernauts, which were like alien Muppets. He spent the last 10 years and most of his income developing the characters and trying to sell the project. What a loser, Chance thinks.

While he didn't rape women, didn't need to as there were plenty of hot women in LA that would sleep with him, the thought of tying them up and taking what he wanted from them aroused Chance more than anything else. He wasn't very rough with most of the women he took home for fear of unleashing something in himself and going too far. He could be rough with the drunk ones since they were less likely to remember what happened. There was one that he did go a little too far with but he didn't let that happen since and she didn't tell anyone.

Even though he slept with good looking women all the time, he could never get the Doctor. He always thought of her as the Doctor but used her name when speaking to her or about her. Deep down he suspected he thought about her that way because he needed a brain doctor but dismissed it as Freudian bullshit. Jungian bullshit?

He really wanted her. *Needed* her. And though he never attempted anything as crazy as this, he thought it was right. He wanted her to be with him voluntarily but, since that didn't happen, he will just take what he wants. Satisfying that way.

He hasn't completely thought of what to do afterwards but he figures that he'll just pay off a cop or claim that she was willing beforehand and didn't like it. Cops will think it is some Me Too garbage and let it go. Besides, he knows at least three people that would lie under oath for him.

Chance mostly told the truth to people, thinking that a lot of people can tell when you are lying, but would sprinkle in lies where needed. He told Billy that Lauren stole $50,000 from him after a night of partying and sex, which was completely untrue, but also told Billy that he would give him half when she returned it, which was true. And people will believe a fat load of bullshit if there is tax-free money in it for them.

How random, he thinks. Someone rammed into the van. Must be someone she knows because people off the street don't do stuff like that in LA. They just don't. This is fucked. He'll have to look into it.

At first, Chance thought, 'hot girl privilege' but then thought, 'who would kidnap a big, fat ugly girl'? Nobody. So no privilege here.

He needed to call the hospital and make sure they sent him Tony's bills. Tony was no genius but he also wasn't stupid. He would keep his mouth shut if the Doctor goes to the police and they find him laid up.

He stood in his Hollywood Hills home, looking out of through the glass sliding doors over the valley below, thinking about what to do next. He'll have to give Billy the 25k at some point but not now. Need to keep the nonsense story up.

3.

Back in the car, James asks, 'Hungry?'

'Getting there. Must be the adrenaline from earlier. It's still pretty early.' Lauren replies. It was maybe 5:30pm? She didn't know and had to look at her watch. 5:42. She was working 12-hour shifts at the hospital and had gotten used to going long spans without eating but now she was starving.

'Ok, we can grab something quick now and go to dinner later?' James asked, hoping for a yes as he drove down the slope of Mission Hills.

'That will work,' Lauren replied, feeling a few things at once. This is nice. Comfortable. Too soon? When did I last brush my teeth? Then realized she was over-thinking. She was extremely intuitive but, like humans do, she over-thought the joy out of everything. She relaxed. But what was she going to wear to dinner and an odd nightclub confrontation? Stop it, brain, she thinks.

The drive on a Friday afternoon was slow, as is driving in Los Angeles at most times, day or night. James looked through the windshield as he drove, only looking over at her at traffic lights or in traffic. He didn't check his phone, like at all. Odd. Lauren split the time looking forward and looking at James, sitting slightly angular so she can see both things without turning her head very much.

James wasn't a very chatty person (typical guy) so Lauren filled in the blank spaces by asking questions. She was VERY curious, as science people naturally are, but a little introverted and didn't normally do all of the talking. A little more introverted these days, in that she felt like it was a progression. She was more outgoing and fun in her junior and senior years of high school, even in her first year of college but got quieter after that. Maybe it was just her workload going through med school that made her quiet but she wasn't sure. It had been a long time since she was fun.

Her best friend Molly was one of those high-energy people that talked all day. She was funny and self-deprecating, cute and a little low on the self-esteem scale but shouldn't be. When they went out together, rarely because of Lauren, they would draw attention from guys, which Molly would intercept with her personality. For that, Lauren was eternally grateful. And so was Molly. She loved the attention. Just a few more years of getting through residency and she would be able to relax and date.

But there is this guy right here...

They talked about childhood and school but not about dating or exes. Nothing too deep, each providing a basic overview of how they got to this point. Surface things. Neither had siblings. Lauren's mother worked in hospital administration and had a PhD that she didn't use anymore. She was in her sixties now, living in Carmel; her parents had children late, focusing on school and careers when they were young. Before his passing, her father was a professor specializing in Global Economics and he had traveled often. She secretly believes he was CIA and tells absolutely everyone confidentially. She doesn't know for sure it but who knows? The passing of Mr. Bradley Parker was a little mysterious.

They talk about clothes for a little while before stopping to grab some tacos and Mexican cokes in glass bottles from El Texate on Pico. The crash weirdly there but far away. James jokes about his winter coat being an insulated hoodie, bridging the conversation from clothes to weather and Lauren tells a story about getting caught in a hailstorm while hiking in Topanga State Park.

They park and head into three stores along the 3rd street promenade, not looking up at the names on signs above the entrances, only in the windows. The first was a little too Boho for Lauren and they moved on. The second store was more modern, had dresses and jeans, tops and a small bag and shoe area. She picked out an LBD, little black dress, for the night and tried it on. It was made from nice material but was simple, which she liked.

When she came out of the dressing room, James thought not for the first time, that she was not just smart but had a great personality and was very attractive as well. Not the typical LA look. No makeup. Long dark hair in just one color. The dress fit perfectly on her. Not surprising, James thought, she's like a size six mannequin.

When he told her how much he liked it, she reached around and tried to get hold of the tag to see how much it cost. She couldn't quite read it so James went to help her. It was $298, which was expensive for most people so James unpinned the tag and said, 'Oh not bad,' and took it. She found casual shoes that were nice enough to go out in and considered some jeans but didn't take them.

'If you like them, get them. I'm picking up the tab so get a few things.' James said. She did, getting the jeans and two tops, one casual and one a little nicer. Lauren didn't look at the prices of anything else after searching for the dress tag, which was unlike her. Her family wasn't rich, not on tough times either, but school had already cost a lot and she still owed some smaller student loans.

She was looking around for a store that sold undergarments but didn't want to announce it. He may have thought that already and brought her to the third store. The third store had underwear and swimsuits, Vans and Converse, watches and casual bags. A unisex skate shop, sort of, with skateboards on the walls and surfboards hanging from the ceiling. They spend some time shopping separately, James keeping an eye on her from the Volcom t-shirt rack or the shoes as she shopped.

She grabbed an armload of stuff to try on, assuming she would buy one or two things, and headed into the changing area. James moved a little closer to that section of the store so he wouldn't be far, assuming they weren't followed or, or what? How would someone track them here? Unless she had a device planted on her. And boy that sounded ridiculous. But what were they really up against? He just didn't know but he thought she might have more of an idea than she was letting on.

She comes out of the changing room wearing jeans and a top and looks at herself in the mirror between the dressing rooms, turning to the side and slightly to the back. James sees her and starts moving that way. He is now further impressed but doesn't want to let it show too much.

'I bet you could put *my* clothes on and make them look good,' he says, walking up.

Lauren cocks her head slightly, the left side of her mouth going up a little. She looks like a cartoon cat about to play with a mouse. 'I'm not sure if that is a compliment or a lame attempt to get me to switch clothes with you,' Lauren replies. 'if that is what you are into.'

He laughs. 'There goes my third date move.'

Lauren laughs out loud at that. When was the last time she had this much fun shopping? Never. She was not the shopping type, for the most part. And were they still in danger? That felt unreal right now.

Lauren thinks, I guess this is a first date now.

James asks, 'What else do you have to try on?'

She looks at the clothes that she collected in the changing room. 'I have a mid-length dress in orange that is not really me, I have a t-shirt and that's about it.'

'You're not going to try on the bikini?' James asks.

A flat look from Lauren. 'Do I seem like the attention-seeking type? I'm actually asking because there is so much of that now.'

Very honestly, James says, 'I didn't ask because I thought you were anything like that. You don't seem like you even have an Instagram account. I was asking purely for selfish reasons.' He shrugs his shoulders, palms up, his face to the side in a 'what-can-you-do-I'm-a-guy look.' She loves it.

'I'll try it on but I'm not wearing it out here. And no, you are not coming in there. I'll take a selfie if it is good.' She said this while looking down somewhat and peeking up, smiling a little. Coy, he thinks.

He grabs a seat and waits as she ducks back into the changing stall. He wouldn't push it if she didn't want to show him. He is quite sure she will look amazing in it. He pulls his phone and checks the news but there isn't anything about the crash. He didn't think there would be but maybe something would be in the local paper, the San Fernando Valley Sun. Nothing.

She's in there for a few minutes and then comes out unannounced in the bikini, which is blue with white and blue Hawaiian flowers on it. James looks up from his phone when she pops out of the stall. He lives near the beach in LA and has seen not just his fair share of beautiful girls in bikinis but probably three times his fair share of beautiful girls in bikinis. She's wearing a standard cut bikini, not overly revealing but still a bikini, but James has temporarily stopped breathing nonetheless. He now fully understands the term 'breath-taking' and has a new appreciation for it.

'I, uhm, that's, fit, good,' he stammers and quickly regains his composure. He walks over and checks the straps to make sure they are not cutting into her shoulders, trying desperately to concentrate on the way the garments fit and not stare and thinks he may have recovered well. Sure.

Smooth, she thinks and laughs a little to herself. She is a pretty shy person and ran out of the dressing cubicle before she had the chance to chicken out.

She also thinks, for the first time, he looked at her not in a gross, leery way, but the way guys look at girls. She is a little disappointed that he has looked at her like *a guy* but also happy he did like a boy, content in knowing that he is not just thinking about having her as a friend or being nice.

'Do you think I should...' Lauren starts.

'I will buy *everything right now.*' James, looking serious, cuts her off in a comical attempt to lighten the mood. He waggled his fingers in a gimmie gesture. 'Give me all of the clothes.'

Lauren grunts out a laugh that wasn't expected. She says, 'No no, I can't let you pay for everything.' She turns to go back and change out of the bikini and he really tries not to look down so he looks up into the same mirror she is looking in and she catches him. They lock eyes for one second, both smiling.

'I would really like to,' he says in a soft voice into the mirror at her, his big, genuine smile disarming. She doesn't feel the floor under her feet for rest of the steps as she ducks back into the changing room. Floating a little.

He doesn't want to try and impress her but feels like he should now, that maybe there should be more to keep her interest. But that is stupid, and he knows it's stupid when he thinks it, but he can't think of anything else at the moment. 'She's a science nerd, remember that,' he thinks to himself and realizes that it helps.

She changes back into her sun dress quickly and comes out of the changing room. She gives him most of the clothes, feeling a little guilty as she does it but they have cute beachy clothes here and she is going to be at the beach. She is also having a lot of fun. She gets some underwear, a few bras, a pair of Flojas flip flops, running shorts, a wooden hair brush that may be organic and seems comically expensive and some sun screen from the small basket by the register. It's too much, she thinks.

James never flinches at the amount of things she has or the price of the items. In fact, he suggests a Hurley zip-up hoodie that matches one of the tops well for when the temperature dips at night, grabs her some socks and suggests a pair of teal Hoka running shoes.

They get over to the register and drop the haul onto the counter. Lauren is about to say something about putting things back when the cashier gives her a 'nice job' smile. Almost a wink. They get out of the store for just over $1,150.

I'm going to need luggage, Lauren thinks.

They are done shopping and head to James' house in Hermosa Beach a few minutes away to get dressed and ready to go out. They don't look completely disheveled but they *feel* like they look disheveled. The slight tension and awkwardness from the fantastic bikini incident was almost gone.

-

'That whole Harvey Weinstein bullshit was wrong,' Chance had said to Billy. Around two years ago, Billy and Chance had gotten drunk together at the Blue Katana but didn't stop drinking when it closed. Chance's driver (he sometimes had one) drove them back to Chance's house in the hills at around 3am and they sat outside in the cooler night air, with Chance smoking cigars and Billy cigarettes. They sipped drinks that had gone from four ingredients to one, being too drunk or too tired to add the rest. Chance's drink, a Rusty Nail, was now just Scotch. Billy's Mojito now just Rum.

'Look,' Chance went on, 'he didn't rape them. He probably fucked a hundred actresses but a couple wanted more money so they came back after him. Bullshit!' he slurred. 'For what? Because they have pussies?'

Billy was nodding, sipping his drink, listening. He was drunk but he was paying attention. He wanted to have powerful friends like this so he kept his mouth shut.

Chance was just getting going. 'What is that for anyway? A pussy. It's for fucking! That's it's *job*! It's made to get a dick in it. They used it to get into a movie and they complain later because they think it shoulda been worth more to fuck that fat slob. Glen Close fucked him but she didn't say shit.'

Billy thought that he had a real point. He chimed in. 'How many people used their bodies to make money? Hookers, laborers, athletes, firefighters. They're not writing white papers for the New England Journal of Medicine. They carry shit, they catch a football.'

'Right! Firefighters are big fuckers. They're made for rescuing people. Pussies are *designed* for fucking! Chance added. 'Even Bill Cosby. I know, I know, some people don't agree because he drugged them. But they all went to his room with him voluntarily,' the last word coming out 'voluntararly'. 'None of them remember shit. He was doing them a favor by knocking them out.'

'I might be pissed if it was my old lady,' Billy thought out loud.

'Why was she going to Bill Cosby's room sober? They were all sober on the way there. For some dick, that's why. She went there for dick, she got dick.'

Billy saw his point. Women weren't accountable for their actions but men were?

Chance asked, 'Let me ask you a question. Sixteen-year-old girls fuck their little boyfriends, right?'

Billy answered, 'All the time.'

'So why is it wrong for a thirty-year-old guy to fuck them? Because our new society says so? Older women want power over their men and they're jealous of young girls. That's why. Older men in power have been fucking sixteen-year-olds since the beginning of time, man. Even up to like seventy-five years ago and no one said shit. That's how it works. Look at what they look like now. They look like grown women with curves and makeup and their ass sticking out of their shorts. That's on purpose. They want to get fucked. They're *supposed* to get fucked.'

Billy wasn't so sure about banging sixteen-year-olds but he thought Chance wasn't wrong. 'I think my grandmother got married at sixteen to a twenty-seven-year-old guy.'

'See! You get it. So I don't care how old she is. She comes here to get fucked, I'm going to fuck her.'

Billy thought again, he's not wrong.

Chance had learned all of this from his father, the man who institutionalized rape.

4.

When they get to James' house in Hermosa, there is not much to look at from the small street that it is on. Two story, four new-looking garage doors on the left side. She thinks it is probably a multi-unit complex. James stops the car in front of the garage door second furthest from the right and gets out, standing in the open car door. He's not in his car so doesn't have a remote opener. He looks around and ducks his head into the car for a second, turning it off.

'I have to go inside to open the door and don't want to leave you out here alone, in case we were followed. This little street is not very busy. Come in.'

He's blocking the garage door next to the one he is pulling into and she hopes the neighbors don't get upset. She follows him around the side of the garage to a small porch in a narrow walking path with a white wood railing and red Adirondack chairs, a white door and blue flowers in planters. Very American with the red, white and blue but beachy. Further along the house is another door almost smothered by a massive Bougainvillea climbing up the side of the house, red flowers everywhere on it.

They go in through the door on the porch into a small living room decorated with weathered wood, a sand beige sofa and chair, lots of wide, white wood molding. Light-to-medium blue paint on the walls. She can see a door on the left and an office on the right with a faux-weathered desk and computer. There is a hallway that might lead to a bedroom and bathroom. It is very New England beachy but looks comfortable at the same time. The couch and chair look comfortable, no hard surfaces showing. Everything is *clean*. Guys aren't this clean.

They head to the left through the door that is steel but doesn't look it, and into the garage. Lauren is a little disappointed at first that she didn't get to see the rest of the small apartment but it dawns on her as she steps through that this isn't a complex. All four garage doors lead to the same space. The first garage bay has gym equipment, the second is empty, third has a Rivian SUV and there is something in the last bay that she can't see behind the Rivian.

Welp, I guess we're not going to upset anyone else by blocking the doors, she thinks. He hits a button and the door at the empty bay starts up. He jumps into the Mercedes and pulls it into the empty bay. She thinks the Rivian looks different than a standard Rivian but can't quite figure out why. She is about to head behind it to see what is lurking behind it but James is out of the wagon with the bags and they're heading back inside. They make a sharp turn when they get inside and head through a door she didn't notice before and up a wooden staircase to the second floor.

The upstairs is well-decorated and cozy. Massive navy blue overstuffed sofa in a fluffy-looking fabric. Walnut hardwood floors. Lighter colors on the walls and moldings. A few interesting, colorful, well-placed art pieces. One painting by Todd White of a woman pouring wine, one a large green canvas painting of seven red wood chairs facing right and one blue chair facing left. Big white kitchen with a seafoam green butler's pantry. The ocean is about two blocks away through the many sliding doors.

'This isn't what I was expecting', Lauren says, pausing in front of the painting of chairs.

'What were you expecting?' James asks. He heads to the refrigerator and raises an eyebrow to Lauren. 'Drink?'

'You said not to get my hopes up so I was expecting one of those small, one bedroom beach houses.' She thinks she understands the chair painting but asks James, 'What attracted you to this?'

James: 'Diet Coke?'

Lauren: 'Sure.'

James stops what he is doing for a minute and looks over. 'That is the artists perception of himself. He's the blue chair facing the wrong way and everyone else is the red chairs.'

Lauren, still studying the painting, thinks about this and says, 'Hmm. I like it.'

She turns from it to look at James again. 'From the outside, I thought it was a multi-unit building. And I didn't expect artwork that would make me think, either.' She peeked down a hallway that led to a lot of doors, some closed, some ajar. 'I could live here for *weeks* and you wouldn't know I was here.'

'Now that is impossible. I notice everything.', James says, pulling two Diet Cokes from the massive Sub-Zero fridge.

'Really?', a challenge in her voice. She closes her eyes. 'What color are my eyes?'

'Hazel', he says without looking at her, no hesitation, cracking open both soda cans.

'Yeah?', she is trying to get him to doubt himself.

'I think they might change color depending on what you are wearing. When I first saw you on the overpass, they were kinda brown but when you were trying on clothes, they were more green.'

'What color were my eyes when I tried on the bikini?' She asks.

James looks at his Diet Coke and says with some gravity and says, 'I have no fucking idea.'

She laughs at the remark but is impressed. She eyes him as she receives the drink. No glass is offered. 'Ok, what color shirt was the huge guy wearing?'

'Black', he says, taking a sip from his can. 'I have wine, if you would like', he offers.

'Not just yet', she replies. 'I think we need to be sharp when we go to the club. I'm impressed with your powers of observation. Most guys wouldn't get the eye question'

'I'm happy that something I can do as a mere mortal can impress you,' James says.

Lauren thinks that there has been a lot of things that impress her so far. She had almost been kidnapped in a white van (cliché!) and he smashed his grandfather's truck to stop it, he knows good tacos, has taken her on a shopping spree and then brought her to this secret villa in

Hermosa Beach, all the while making her feel, surprisingly, not worried in the slightest about him being a total stranger.

They get changed into their nightclub clothes in separate bathrooms. The spare bathroom, James informs her, has new toothbrushes, toothpaste, hair machines, soap and deodorant under the sink.

'Do you have a lot of unexpected female company that is in need of extra toothbrushes, Jimmy?' she asks, jokingly.

James: 'The package is new,' he says reassuringly, but adds 'The fifty-pack ran out so I had to get more.' He smiles.

'Uh huh. Sure, jocular!' She calls back. Lauren could hear the smile in the comment he made but looks on Amazon quickly to see if they sell a fifty-pack of toothbrushes... and sonofabitch they do! She'll have to think about this.

James took a shower and dressed in casual pants the color of charcoal, a whitish casual dress shirt with a pattern of tiny bathtubs on it that is cut square at the bottom so it doesn't get tucked in and a pair of nicer Vans.

His hair looks freshly shaped again but slightly messy, but intentionally messy.

Lauren puts on the little black dress with tight black yoga shorts underneath and the casual shoes she bought. She curls her hair around the front, a quick job to make it look presentable. She was going to do more but was suddenly exhausted, probably from the adrenaline dump earlier.

'Is there time for a nap?', she asks James, half jokingly.

'Oh my god there is always time for a nap,' is his response. He tells Alexa to play some classical piano and, even though she thinks she won't sleep, she falls asleep quickly on the couch with a throw blanket. James sits and closes his eyes but doesn't doze. He just thinks. And peeks at Lauren every so often.

5.

When Chance was growing up and learning computers, he met a lot of people in chat rooms. Chat rooms were big for computer nerds then. Not like MySpace, where everyone posted public pictures and songs and words to songs and poems or like Facebook, where people posted what they did the night before or pictures of food. Old school chat rooms were where you went with a handle only, no pictures, no locations, met other nerds and talked shit.

This was also where a person got things done on the internet. Need software? Someone in your group has an unlicensed version available. Need to get in somewhere? Ask around and the network will find a way. These were real hackers, the tech folks that worked at the tech giants and phone companies. At Ticketmaster. At the DMV. They could get you into most things and places for free because you would repay them in kind. And if something did need payment, Bitcoin was favored.

Chance's online personality, unchanged since he was sixteen, suggested that he was a child of a single, immigrant dad but without a lot of money. He used this to keep the price of things reasonable. If the community thought that he was well off, they would charge him large fees for everything. So he logs in under his handle (Anonimouse) and pings Kaytea (he thinks it may be KT, initials for something), another hacker who has gotten him into the DMV before.

He tells Kaytea that his dad used to own a Triumph Spitfire when he was young but sold it when he had kids and he'd like to find one near Sacramento, his made-up hometown. Chance knows that they are not overly expensive like most old cars and claims he wants to buy one for his dad, who probably doesn't have a lot of time left, but can't find one for sale.

In reality, his dad was suffering from memory loss and was stored away in the lockdown level at a home for seniors. His driving days were over.

Kaytea likes the story and two hours later gets him a login and password for the California DMV that will work until Monday morning.

He thanks her profusely and promises to help her if she needs anything, and logs off.

He pulls out his hacking machine, a laptop he made with components bought from Fry's (R.I.P. Fry's, he thinks) and boots it up. He connects it to a burner phone that he ordered online with a Missouri phone number and goes to work. He knows that the cell phone emits a radio transmission to a cell tower that logs the call but the DMV login was created by an administrator and is legitimate. Besides, there is no way to trace who bought any of the equipment even if the DMV finds out about the entry. He won't be editing any of the DMV database information so there won't be a changelog entry either.

Chance runs a query on Dodge Power Wagons in the Los Angeles area, which turns up three. A blue one in Fontana, somewhere around 60 miles from the pick-up, one registered NonOp, or non-operational, in Monrovia, and the third, an orange one in West Hills, 5 miles from the pickup. Hello Crash Bandicoot.

He writes down the name and address of the Willis Family Trust in West Hills, California. Not sure what he will do with that just yet but good to have. Maybe he'll call on Billy again. He didn't have a lot of people he trusted for something like this but it might be too much for Bill.

-

Billy is alone in his car outside of Lauren's massive apartment complex, scrolling through his phone but not really looking at it. Looking past it at the door. Nothing so far. He probably shouldn't be here in case someone saw him earlier but it's pretty dark now and no one will really be able to see him well.

He knows Chance's story is probably bullshit but he figures Chance isn't going to clearly say what kind of shenanigans he is up to. Billy can interpret his motives. If he reports in and lets him know that he found her, he might give him a little extra. And maybe a turn with the girl...

Another half hour and he calls it. She's either already inside the complex or she isn't going to risk coming back here today. It's a dangerous pick-up site anyway with young people coming and going at all hours.

He'll take a shower and get over to the club. He could use a drink or three to loosen up his tightening muscles.

6.

James and Lauren go to the Blue Katana and order drinks. They ask the bartender, a short, hot model/actress/bartender in a low-cut shirt, if Chance is around but she says she doesn't know, since the office has a separate entrance. They walk to a small, white counter-height table with two white chairs facing each other. They search around the not-very-busy club, checking the faces of everyone in the crowd for mostly no reason while they talk about high school and college experiences, keeping the conversation light. But Chance doesn't come in for the hour and a half that they are there.

-

Billy takes a hot shower and lets the water go to work on his neck and shoulders. He was ready for the impact when the pickup hit the van, which helped, but not completely. He feels like he was in the gym trying to lift more than normal, every muscle aching.

Out of the shower and dressed in his going-out clothes of a blue button-up shirt with small red dots and gray khakis, he eats four Advil and slicks his hair back. He's going to have to change that style or he will be all forehead soon. Short and bald is not a good look. He goes down to his car, an aging BMW 3 Series, and heads to the Blue Katana.

He says hello to Keith at the door and heads in. He takes a seat at the bar and orders a vodka club with a lime from Misty, who is on early. He's grateful for that because Misty has the nicest body of all the bartenders here. She doesn't talk much and doesn't complain if she catches him checking her out. Perfect, he thinks.

As he is trying not to get caught staring at Misty, he's looking in the mirror behind the bar when he sees Lauren at a high top table with (he thinks) the pickup driver. He looks away quickly in case they recognize him but they grab a table and sit. The guy is a little off to the side and not looking directly at Billy in the mirror, which is good since he just saw Billy that way a few hours ago.

What are the chances that it's a coincidence? None, of course. There is zero chance that they just wound up here tonight. They don't seem to recognize him from the crash. That's good. But that means she either recognized Tony or thinks that Chance had something to do with it. That's not good.

-

James and Lauren leave the Blue Katana and go to Sharkees on the pier in Hermosa near James' house, a fun, super-busy bar with half-price, low alcohol shots and a DJ. It has probably been semi-crowded since happy hour and will probably get more crowded as the night goes on.

When they get tired of yelling at each other in Sharkees over the club-version of the Macarena (is everyone yelling, 'Aaay Macarena' or was that just the song? They couldn't tell since it seemed the noise was coming from everywhere), they leave and go a few doors down to the Brittania Arms, an English-style pub with 7 customers, stinky old carpet and classic rock on the juke box. James feeds it a $20 bill and plays 'How Soon Is Now?' by the Smiths and a few other songs. They grab a few pints from the bar and huddle into a corner.

The conversation turned to what are they going to do next. Did they really think about what would happen at the Blue Katana? What would they have said to Chance? Would they get pulled into a back room?

The only thing they know for sure is that they should be more careful going forward. They could have gotten into more trouble. And they will probably have to tell the police an edited version of the story.

They go back to James' place after a few beers at the bar and talk for a while, drinking large glasses of ice water. They talk on the couch, the balcony, the gazebo on the roof, which has a bar they don't drink from, a couch they don't sit on and a hot tub that they don't go in. They talk about childhood, music, pets. Anything. Everything. They fall asleep together on the massive blue sectional in the living room, lying on their sides, fully clothed, her head close to his. When her breathing becomes steady, he gets up and grabs a couple of off-white chunky throws from a rack, puts one on her and lays back down with the other.

-

As Billy follows them from the Blue Katana, he says, 'This is too easy,' to the empty car. He talks to himself a lot and thoroughly enjoys it. In the world of hands-free phones in cars and almost invisible ear buds, no one notices. He sees them turn onto a small street and stop in front of a garage door but he keeps moving on the bigger avenue, noting the location and finding a parking spot.

7.

They wake up when the sun comes through the upper, shadeless rectangular windows, which is around 9:30. James thinks that it may be too late for Ella's. 'Throw on some clothes and a hat, we need to get to Ella's,' James tells Lauren without any context. They scramble around, getting ready (Lauren thinking 'who is Ella?' while she is brushing her teeth, eyeing the toothbrush again and thinking, fifty pack?), and walk three blocks to a small, local coffee shop for breakfast.

It is not warm at the beach in the morning and they are both wearing hoodies. Hers is the Hurley from store two over cargo pants and a new black top she got at store one yesterday. The Hokas and her ponytail run through a blue baseball hat with a white B on it that she borrowed completing the look.

James puts on khakis and a t-shirt, taking a few minutes to fix his hair and brush his teeth.

They make it before the line forms, for which James is grateful. Usually by 9:30 on a weekend there are a few people queued up waiting for a table but not today. Despite the chilly breeze, a perky blonde in tiny shorts and tiny top greets them with a smile and says, 'Hey James. Two?' James nods and replies, 'Hey Jules,' and she leads them to a small table. They order coffees and orange juices and check out the laminated menu.

Lauren thinks James comes here a lot.

James: 'We didn't come to a final decision last night. Are you staying for a while?'

Lauren: 'If that is okay with you, yes. I'm still a little freaked, like part of me still doesn't believe it.'

James: 'So I can stop sucking in my gut now?'

'Gut? Oh, you're not going to be one of those high maintenance guys that is going to fish for compliments all the time, are you?', Lauren says in mock exasperation.

'That depends. Do I look good on these fishing trips?', he laughs.

'Lordy', she says, smiling.

-

Saturday is relatively quiet. In comparison to Friday, Lauren thinks, a rock concert in Vegas would be quiet. They spend most of the day walking, talking and eating, deciding on a movie later that afternoon. The girl part of Lauren's very analytical brain is thinking that this must be an act. There is no way this rich (no one has a house like that and isn't rich), funny, good looking guy is single and not damaged in some way.

But as they go along, she gets the feeling he has been overlooked somehow by his generation. Since he doesn't really party (or says he doesn't) or play a sport of some kind or interact with other humans, it seems, that maybe he doesn't belong with the people his age. So, while walking along the promenade next to the Pacific Ocean, she asks.

'So who do you normally hang out with?' Lauren asks.

'I've got some friends that I play volleyball with on the beach. Right there in fact,' he says, pointing out some busy volleyball courts in the sand.

Lauren looks over at the scene and thinks that it looks like a cologne ad. Beautiful, fit people in very small athletic wear hitting a ball back and forth in a well-choreographed-looking rally. It just needs to be in black and white and have some slow-motion shots after the points.

Snapping her back to the present, James continues, 'I play cards sometimes with a group of guys, other property owners and developers.

They're friends that I work with. We deal with each other on certain properties too, but we're not so friendly at card games. Those are more ruthless.'

'Ruthless?', Lauren asks, eyebrows raised, thinking that high stakes poker seems like it could be his vice. Maybe Vegas trips.

'Yeah. Morty will cheat at cards but never at business. They all cheat, except for Davis, I think.'

'Wait, they cheat and this doesn't bother you?', she pauses, 'And you have a friend named Morty? How old are these people?'

'It's a one hundred dollar buy in, no re-buys. Morty is the oldest at seventy, I think. The rest are in their late fifties or early sixties,' James says.

'Oh,' she says. Probably not the high stakes, all out Vegas she was thinking.

'They're not like super old. Morty still does triathlons, most play squash and they all play golf,' James says, justifying himself.

'No judgement, I like older people too. They have less bullshit,' Lauren notes.

'I play games online with a couple of old friends from LA sometimes and I go out with some high school people on occasion for beers. I have a few friends in the neighborhood here I see around. What about you?'

Lauren says, 'I have my best friend Molly that I told you about. She's about the only one I go out with. Then there is Phyllis at work who I talk to a lot. There's Matty, who likes to shop and gossip. And I hang out with my mom when she comes down.'

'Is it Maddy, like Madison or Matty, like Matthew?'

'Jealous?' she asks.

James says, 'Nope. You didn't know I existed until now so I'm sure any retreads or friends-with-benefits situationships will seem ridiculous now.' Sounding over-confident, but light-hearted.

'Friends in the neighborhood, like Jules?' asks Lauren. She would have one eyebrow raised, if she could raise only one eyebrow.

James nods. 'Yeah, exactly. I have a lot of those.'

-

That night, they sleep in James' bed, her in a set of his pajamas that look new and him in running shorts and a loose workout shirt. There is a window open, allowing cool, salty air and intermittent roar of the ocean to come through.

They spoon but nothing more. Lauren feels his strong arm around her and feels safe. She didn't think she felt unsafe before but she feels like maybe she was on edge or something before and didn't know it. She didn't realize that she needed someone to be there for her.

It takes a while for her to fall asleep. Right before she dozes, she thinks, 'He's such a gentleman that I'm going to have to instigate the sex...' and the thought of the comfortable spooning after sex lulls her to sleep.

-

The next morning, James hops out of bed early and tells Lauren he's going to the garage to work out. When he asks if she'd like to join, she declines, opting to stay ensconced in the soft sheets and fluffy blankets. When he heads down, she pulls her phone and texts Molly to update her on what is happening.

After the first few texts (Lauren likes to start with 'U up?' and Molly makes fun of her for not knowing that is a booty call), Lauren writes, 'So I met this guy,' and hits send. She's about to write more when Molly calls. When Lauren picks up, Molly is already talking.

'I can't believe you haven't sent me a picture yet. When did this happen? What does he look like?' she says before Lauren can say hello.

Molly has always had the ability to stream off words at a furious pace, never pausing for a second to edit what she is about to say. Lauren has always been slightly afraid of what might come out of her mouth in a public setting and attributes Molly's brain-to-mouth speed as a kind of higher intelligence.

She laughs at the Molly rapid-fire and replies, 'I'm a terrible friend,' and tells her the story.

Molly listens, only interjecting, 'Shut the front door!' or 'No flippin' way!' or even 'Cheese and rice!' at the highlights. When Lauren is done, she asks, 'He took you shopping?'

'Molly, how is that all you got from this story? I'm the most boring friend you have! Nothing *ever* happens to me but I almost get *kidnapped* and you focus in on *shopping*?'

'That's an average weekend for me,' Molly says lightly and chuckles. 'Not the shopping part though. No man has ever volunteered to take *me* shopping.'

Lauren laughs and replies, 'You haven't met one that can afford to take you shopping yet.'

Molly: 'So where are you?'

Lauren, in a softer voice: 'In his bed in Hermosa Beach. Wearing his pajamas.'

Molly: 'You slut! Good for you. About time you used that thing. Did it hurt? Were you rusty?'

Lauren: 'We haven't done it yet. He's being a gen...'

But Molly cuts her off, booing into the phone at her. They both laugh.

Molly: 'That sounds more like you. You know what you need to do? You need to lie to me more often. Make these stories more *interesting*.'

Lauren: 'I'm a scientist, not a writer. You should take my boring stories and re-write them so they're more fun. Publish them, maybe.'

Molly: 'I could probably write a good story based on my life but I am not creative enough to make one of your stories readable.'

-

James showers after his hour-long workout and they have coffee at James' kitchen island but neither are very hungry this morning. They dress in shorts and casual shirts and make plans to walk down the beach.

As is usual for mid-day, there are only one or two surfers out, and they are mostly people trying to learn on the small waves. James and Lauren chat while carrying their shoes, Lauren with flip flops and James with some kind of water shoe.

James mentions his girlfriend from high school and her betrayal. Lauren listens, keeping quiet, noting how much older he sounds when talking about it.

When he stops, she only says, 'Well, lucky me, then,' and gives him a big smile.

They stop for lunch at a beach-themed pizza restaurant, on the beach of all places, and the topic of sex came up, but not by accident.

'So James, what is your type?' Lauren asked.

'Furries,' James says quickly, straight-faced.

Lauren covers her mouth to prevent herself from snorting a laugh. 'Seriously,' she asks when she composes herself. 'What have your exes looked like?'

James is smiling and Lauren knows he's going to keep going. 'Small frame, dark hair, hazel eyes, just like mom,' James says, describing Lauren.

'Horrifying,' Lauren says and smiles. 'No, seriously!'

'I don't have a type. I'm not into blondes or Asians or anything like that in particular,' he says between bites of pizza and shrugs.

'Uh huh. I bet all of those toothbrush users looked the same.'

'Honestly, I don't think that a particular type attracts me. I think some people are attractive because of who they are and how they are. I wouldn't be more attracted to you if you had blue eyes. I think you are perfect the way you are.'

Lauren looks at him and thinks, damn, he always has the right answer. Let's test that. 'Ok, so what do you like sex-wise?'

'I like it when girls enjoy it, when they're into it. Like I would want you to enjoy yourself many times before I do the first time. But THIS is where things get sexist.'

Lauren crinkles her eyebrows. 'What do you mean?'

'Ok', James says, putting down his crust. 'A guy and a girl go off to have sex for the first time. Most of the time, she doesn't tell him what she likes beforehand but has some sort of expectation of what will happen. Like as if we know what makes you, you know, click. But we don't really know anything. I know the basic anatomy stuff but maybe you're into getting tied up. I wouldn't have a clue. And if I start tying you up on our third date, you might call the police. But if you leave the experience unsatisfied, you tell other people and we look bad. That's not cool.'

Lauren thinks about it. 'You're right. It is one-sided. To avoid that from happening here,' she waggles a finger between them, 'I should probably tell you what I like and don't like. But it's been a while for me so we may have to do a trial-and-error system...'

'A scientific approach then,' James says through a smile, thoughts rushing through his brain.

'Precisely' she replies.

'This may take a while. We should get started as soon as possible.'

8.

Lauren takes off for two weeks and stays with James at his insistence, saying that he can't protect her if she isn't with him. It might a little unnecessary, since they know nothing about the threat to her, but she doesn't think so. Also, they were having a great time.

He goes to her apartment alone that Sunday to get clothes and supplies, thinking about computers and chargers, makeup, clothes. He packs most of everything that doesn't look neglected there, leaving her in the company of Edgar, his mechanical engineer friend.

Edgar is a Portuguese man in gray coveralls with a round face and pokey hair that nicely tries to explain things to Lauren as if he hasn't met a smart woman before. She is thinking that he might be on the spectrum. James neglects to tell Edgar that she is one of the smartest people he has met.

Besides thinking that Edgar *may* have social issues, she has also found out that he has modified James' Rivian with solar panels and coils on the wheels that generate energy like an alternator. Or something like that. Between that and capturing brake energy, the Rivian never needs charging, he says.

The car she couldn't see behind the Rivian is an Aston Martin. She is not sure of what model it is but it looks new and silver and as sexy as *hell* and adds a whole new dimension to old-pickup-driving, super-nice James, who also still drives his mom's station wagon. Something a little dangerous, a little spy-like. Maybe that is James Bond thinking (she has only seen one, Skyfall, but she liked it). She tells James later, 'That car is an oxymoron. You seem like the safest person in the world.'

'Ah,' James says, 'I like to go very fast, just safely.'

Lauren eyes him with a little mischievous curiosity. She likes that he is not one-dimensional and wants to go for a ride in that Aston.

-

Lauren and Edgar chat in the downstairs apartment waiting for James to get back. When James comes in from the garage carrying three bags, Lauren starts to cry a little. James stops and says, 'I'm sorry, did you not want me to use these bags?' which might be the goofiest thing she has ever heard but he's so sweet that she laughs a little through the tears. What she was upset about was that her whole life was packed into these three bags and that she now felt homeless, completely dependent on this almost-stranger, after going to med school and creating her own independent life for herself.

It almost feels like a trap. This cute guy doing all of these great things, which is awesome and a little unbelievable at times, and losing the independence that she has made for herself feels wrong. But great.? 'It can't be true,' part of her brain says to her. 'This doesn't happen in real life.'

'I'm okay, just a little uncomfortable having to depend on someone else.'

Edgar excuses himself and retreats to a small workbench in the garage, clearly uncomfortable with feelings.

Lauren asks about the traffic, which is always an LA conversation, to change the subject. James shrugs as if he didn't notice any and puts the bags down in the first floor living room. He unplugs his laptop and offers Lauren the first floor apartment for privacy, since they just met.

'You just don't want to carry those bags upstairs, huh?', Lauren says.

James is shaking his head halfway through this question like he is going to disagree with her, but says seriously 'Fuck no', smiles, and picks the bags back up and heads for the stairs.

Lauren laughs and thinks that tension that could have been between them at that moment was thoroughly diffused. They're practically strangers, her almost getting kidnapped and him with the daring rescue. He's moving her stuff in for God's sake. But, when things could have been the most tense, they made jokes and laughed.

'It's temporary, brain,' she reminds herself, and wonders about that.

-

James takes Lauren out to an early dinner at an inexpensive seafood restaurant on the beach. Since it is too late for lunch and too early for dinner, the restaurant isn't busy. The hostess, a mid-twenties Asian girl wearing a bikini, sandals and see-through wrap, twiddles her fingers at them as they walk in and says, 'Hi James!' She grabs two menus and says, 'Inside or outside?'

'Outside, please. Thanks Kira,' James says and they follow her out to the large, wraparound deck.

Kira smiles at Lauren and looks at James for a beat as she sets down the laminated menus and says, 'Enjoy', heading back to the hostess stand.

Lauren looks after her and then at James, who smiles and says, 'What?'

While on the surface she feels that this is going well, despite all of the attractive, semi-clad girls James knows, Lauren is a little nervous. Not about James but about the kidnapping.

She wasn't aware of it before but she catches herself now looking around and not at the menu. How many times had she done this? As a Neuroscientist, she should have expected a range of reactions regarding the attempted kidnapping but has been wrapped up in the storybook romance of the cute athletic guy saving the damsel in distress.

Her brow crinkles as she thinks of this. When it does, James catches it and asks, 'Not finding anything? We can go somewhere else.'

She looks up and begins to explain to him that she is experiencing a little panic but sees the small, knowing smile on his face and stops.

'If it is any consolation, it is my first time rescuing a beautiful woman from the clutches of dastardly men too.' Lauren opens her mouth to explain her feelings but stumbles when he says the words "beautiful' and 'dastardly' and just smiles. James waits.

She puts down her menu and says sincerely, 'Thank you.' James smirks a little, as if there is no reason for thanks. Lauren shakes it off continues, 'No, I need to acknowledge what you have done for me. I could have been raped or killed. You saved me, you saved my *life.* So thank you. You are an amazing person for that act alone.'

She adds, 'I'm scared. I don't know when I was this scared before. If ever.'

James waits a beat to make sure she's gotten it off her chest and says, 'Do you believe in fate, or destiny?'

Lauren, on the verge of tears but doesn't want to be 'a girl', shakes her head.

'Ok, I don't either. This may sound weird but I think we're in control of our fate. I think we're not all we appear to be on the surface. You studied the brain. Do you know what the human brain is capable of?

She shakes her head again but the conversation is diluting the choked up feeling she had a few minutes ago. He has brought her into her comfort zone and she makes a mental note of it. He's clever, and she brightens because she's more comfortable with the conversation and because he did that.

'Right?', James continues, 'What if we're, not telekinetic, but able to shape the world around us to some extent? I read somewhere that a large part of us is made up from stardust. Like 86% of stuff from other planets or Big Bang parts. Maybe that is where it comes from.'

The waitress shows up at this exact moment, when neither of them had expected. 'Hi, I'm Candi and I'll...oh hey James', she says, smiling.

Candi, wearing a bikini top of small, orange triangles with white cutoff shorts that highlight her dark skin, doesn't need a notepad for orders. On her feet are ankle socks and $900 Christian Louboutin tennis shoes. Her face is freckled across the bridge of her dark nose.

'Hey Candi! Can we have two margaritas to start with? Cadillacs?' James asks.

Candi squats next to Lauren and looks her square in the face. She smiles. She turns to James and says, 'Of course. Are you going to introduce me to your lovely friend or do I have to be that person?'

Without waiting, she puts her hand out and says, 'Hi, I'm Candice. I'm sorry my friend is so rude. What is your name?'

A little shy, Lauren shakes the outstretched hand and says, 'Lauren. Nice to meet you, Candi.' They shake and Candi gives James a sidelong look. She says, 'Don't screw this one up,' and is up on her way with a grace that makes Lauren think Candi is a ballerina.

Lauren gives James a flat look. James, palms up in a shrug, says, 'My friends. Where were we? Oh right. What if our extra sensory power is making our lives what they are?'

'I love where you are going with this conversation but I have to ask, what is her deal? She looks like she should be laying by the pool at the Beverly Hilton or whatever it is that rich girls do.'

'Candi is a model, a very popular model,' James adds. 'I don't think she needs this job but she brings in a lot of customers. Like scouts and photographers. She might own this place now.'

Shaking off the unbelievable difference between their two lives, Lauren continues the topic of telepathy. 'I love the mystery behind science, especially brain science. We know how it works, like electrical impulses, behaviors, the need to reproduce, but there is so much we don't know.'

She realized that she's animated now, hands moving, eyes bright, and that she had completely forgot about being scared. As the gigantic frozen margaritas were being placed on the table by the lovely Candice, she thought, damn, he completely distracted me.

The Doctor thing is starting to grind at Chance. It keeps bugging him. He gets obsessive and he thinks that would normally be a problem for most people but not for him. That's how he got where he is, he thinks. That's how successful people make things happen.

He did almost get in trouble once with that actress from the popular CW show. Kristine something? It made him mad every now and again that he had to pay her off. What a waste of money. And he didn't get to finish what he started.

But she didn't press charges and the story didn't leak.

It's amazing that Billy found them in Hermosa Beach, especially since the West Hills address was a lawyer's office. He thinks that he probably got away with it but can't guarantee that everyone will keep their mouth shut.

Plus, he wants her more now. He's been getting more, vigorous, with the girls he has been bringing home from the club but not as vigorous as he would like. He would like to punish Lauren for a while...

He thinks about what to do next and considers inviting her to his place in the Hollywood hills. He then thinks that is the worst idea he's ever had and tries to block her out. He tries to focus on his latest project, a low budget horror movie that might make a big profit but can't seem to keep that going.

He puts on porn but winds up looking at shorter brunettes and thinks about her again. So he finds one of a cute brunette getting tied up and used by several guys and takes care of himself. He's angry at the end of it, feeling like he was played somehow by her.

He calls Billy and tells him to see if he can get her someplace isolated.

9.

How safe is too safe?

After two weeks of being on vacation with a total stranger, as Lauren has categorized it, and everything going fantastically well, Lauren decides it is time to return to work. James tells her that she can take as long as she likes, which sounds like a wonderful break to Lauren after med school and her ongoing residency, but she needs to go back. She is still thinking that this situation is not real, that this great guy who is sweet and in perfect shape has to have bodies hidden somewhere. Like a huge walk-in closet full of skeletons. She just can't seem to find them though.

So James drives her to work every day and picks her up every day.

After a month, Lauren goes to work alone in the Rivian, as James wouldn't let her take her Kia.

-

Billy thinks Lauren has seen her looking at him while he is tailing her and Young Matt Damon, as Billy has come to think of James, but maybe doesn't recognize him. So, driving a rented Hyundai and wearing scrubs he saved from a TV show he was in briefly (called Scrubs, of all things), he cruises the up-close employee lot where the doctors park, expecting to catch the drop off, and idles near a red zone.

Surprised, he sees the Rivian come into the lot and park. He hurriedly pulls into a hatch-marked non-spot across from her in the employee section. He pulls his gun out from a holster he wedged between the seats, sticks it in a front pocket, gets out and walks towards her as she is getting out of the Rivian.

What he sees looks like recognition but he isn't sure if she knows who he is (from the bar? From movies? From Scrubs?) or if she has seen him tailing her. With her new taser in her bag, she reaches her right hand inside for it (the entire time she is thinking about ponchos flying up like a scene from a western like 'The Good, The Bad and The Ugly') but Billy is already bringing up the gun from his pocket and shoots her twice in the stomach before she has time to draw the taser.

He wasn't supposed to shoot her. He was just going to point it at her and make her get in the car.

'That's so unfair', she thinks, before her legs fail and she sits sideways to the left, right hand still trying to pull the taser out of the inside pocket of her bag.

-

Nelson, a Filipino nurse, had just gotten off shift and was texting his newest distraction, Travis the Man Slut as he calls him, from his Prius in the parking lot. For about ten minutes, they text about how Travis thinks that people who drive a Toyota Prius don't like to drive. Travis isn't wrong about the Prius thing but Nelson likes to act appalled and Travis likes the attention.

He sends several short texts because he thinks Travis wouldn't read a long text. As he is thinking that ten words if too long for Travis' attention span, he hears two balloons pop behind his car.

-

Billy sees movement but doesn't turn to look at it because that would give the observer a straight look at his face. He walks normally to the Hyundai, adjusts his fake glasses and drives off out of the parking lot at a reasonable speed for someone who just finished a shift.

'Fuck fuck fuck fuck,' he thinks while driving away.

-

Nelson looks in his windshield rear view a second after he hears the pops and the person he sees shows no reaction to the noise, just keeps walking. Maybe it was just him? Is the radio on? He checks. Nope. He sees the Hyundai back out and drive off, not running fast so he isn't worried that there might be an active shooter. He thinks he probably wouldn't know a gunshot from a hole in the ground. Phone still in hand, he puts his car in reverse to back out of the spot and sees someone on the ground in the backup camera, partially underneath a car parked behind him to the left.

He forgets about Travis the Man Slut and calls Latrisha, an ER nurse and his friend who is, thankfully, on shift at the hospital.

Latrisha is a get-shit-done person. She is actually 'the' get-shit-done person at Mission Hills Hospital. When Latrisha is activated into emergency response mode, everyone else stands by to assist and absolutely no one interferes. Not family members, not orderlies, not doctors.

Latrisha Smith is an intense woman when she needs to be, which is most of the time. She works out like an athlete, drinks alcohol like an Irish fish and laughs as often as possible. Her parents both died young and she figures that she will as well so she lives life to the fullest.

-

Phone still in hand, Nelson jumps from his car and runs to the writhing Lauren. 'I'm Nelson and I'm going to help you,' he says to Lauren, completely in first-responder mode. 'Let me see your wound.' He moves Lauren's left hand, takes a look and puts it back. He calls Trish's personal cell, which she answers on the second ring. He quickly briefs her on what he sees while he kneels next to Lauren. He says to Lauren, 'I've seen worse, Boo. You will be fine.'

-

Trish moves out from behind an ER nurse's station (they want her to call it the Emergency Department but she is not referring to the place she works at as the ED) and grabs two paramedics and their gurney from the hall they are walking through towards their truck. She tells one to grab bandages because they have a gunshot wound to the abdomen, which he does immediately.

She sees Dr. Morehouse heading to the doctor's lounge with his food and tells him, let's go, that one of theirs has been shot in the employee lot, which he does instantly, setting his tray on the floor and turning to follow.

Trish, walking fast, hits the employee parking lot door with 5 people in her wake that she has collected along her way. Dr. Morehouse, 2 EMTs, a transportation orderly and the security guard at the employee entrance. She looks around quickly to see if the shooter is still around and tells the guard to keep lookout.

Trish knows Lauren in a 'I know she works here' way and is somewhat shocked to see that it is her but heard about the attempted kidnapping so not completely so. The EMTs talk to Lauren and apply some gauze to stop the bleeding, getting her on a stretcher and rolling her in to the hospital within 2 minutes. Only one exit wound. Lauren asks Trish to call James but Trish tells her that, unless James is an anesthesiologist, she doesn't need James there right now but she will call him when she can.

The is an open operating room and they roll Lauren right in. The EMT's transfer Lauren to an operating table and continue to check her vitals while Dr. Morehouse and Nelson are there connecting Lauren to an IV and giving her pain medication. The OR nurse and Trish search for the anesthesiologist and surgeon that are on duty.

The anesthesiologist arrives first and asks Lauren questions about allergies and asks what pain meds were given. He leaves and comes back in a few minutes with something to knock her out with.

The OR nurse hangs up a phone and says, 'Surgeon is 2 minutes out.'

The anesthetic goes into the IV and Lauren says 'Thaaa' and is asleep under the mask in the OR.

Trish calls the 4th floor where Lauren works and talks to Alejandra, who has worked on 4 since the ice age and knows everyone. Allie calls Phyllis, who has James' number, which she gives to Mike in HR, who calls James. James quickly grabs some things like toothpaste, deodorant, some gym clothes, tosses them in a gym bag and gets in the Aston Martin.

He doesn't have her mom's number and calls Mike back. Mike has already called Lauren's mother Victoria four times, giving her real-time updates on her condition and providing James' number.

The forty-eight-minute drive takes James thirty-three minutes.

Victoria calls. 'Tori, please', she says, and asks what happened. James tells her the attempted kidnapping story, the weeks at the Hermosa house, the return to work. Tori knew most of it from Lauren but James doesn't know exactly what she has heard and tells it all. Tori thanks James and tells him to text or call with updates. He apologizes to her for letting his guard down and that it will never happen again, but she knows that there was no way to know that this would happen. She tells him that he is a victim too, not at fault.

-

The surgery takes two and a half hours. They recover one bullet, stitch up her upper and lower intestines and skin. Although the surgeries are extensive, Lauren is a healthy twenty-eight-year-old woman and should have no problem recovering.

When they admit Lauren to the recovery ward after the operations, they do it under the name Harriett Smith, Latrisha's grandmother.

-

James tells Tori that the hospital won't give out any information about Lauren to anyone who calls and Tori thinks that is for the best. She knows her daughter is alive and will do fine but is on edge. She only managed to have the one baby go full term after all the tries and is shaken that she was almost taken away. She feels like she needs to tell someone else, to talk to someone just to vent off some of the stress and calls her friend Lula in She texts James that she'll be down tomorrow to visit Harriett.

-

Billy calls the hospital to find out what room Lauren Parker is in. After going through several layers of machines, he finds out from a human that the hospital doesn't have anyone by that name. He thinks she didn't make it and thinks about what he is going to say to Chance. But Chance doesn't know that Billy shot her or that Billy was even following her so he just won't say anything about it.

If she died, which he thinks she did, he might not get any money from Chance but at least she wouldn't be able to identify him. If she's alive, he has a new problem.

-

James calls a friend and gets 24-hour security to Lauren's room. The security is mostly ex-police and military guys, all personable and all smart. The eyes, James thinks, when he is talking to them. The eyes never turn off. Even the chubby retired officer from Santa Clarita can be mid-story, animated and bright in the way people get when remembering/telling a great story, will still be tracking movement, looking for threats.

James stays with her at the hospital for five days, only going home to shower and change, picking up treats for the nursing staff on the way back. They bring him a cot to sleep on, sometimes a recliner, a bedside table to work on and as much hospital food as he can eat. He brings them boxes of delicious things from the bakery in the mornings, salads and pastas from a restaurant and desserts from a variety of places. The nurses love him and love Lauren, who they thought was nice before but are a little jealous of her now. Happy for her, but not 100%...

10.

The day after the shooting, Tori Parker comes to the hospital to visit Lauren/Harriett. She is witty and elegant, well dressed without being overdressed, a little humility peeking through the glamour at times. James is captivated by her, talking to her for hours, listening to stories. Lauren is happy to have her there, comforted in the knowledge that her mom is with her and that these two are getting along so well. Maybe too well?

'Mom,' she says on her third day in the hospital, 'lay off the charm. You're setting the bar too high for me,' partially joking.

'You don't want him to think we get boring when we get older, do you? Besides, there is no bar for him anymore. My diagnosis from my first phone conversation with him is that I couldn't run him off if I wanted to. You have him smitten.'

James has offered Tori the downstairs apartment in Hermosa or his parent's house five minutes away from the hospital (where he has been showering) but she gracefully declines, stating that she is staying with friends in La Cañada Flintridge. She may take him up on it when Lauren goes back to James' house though.

Lauren, who wasn't sure what she wanted to do next, is somewhat put out by this statement but at the same time is aware that she doesn't have a lot of options. She thought staying with mom in Carmel might be a good place to go but now isn't sure. Could they find me there? And then, triumphantly, thinks, 'I have officially faked my own death!'

-

The police came to get a statement, first from James on day one and then from Lauren on day two, but she was asleep. James told them about the attempted kidnapping, leaving out the crash, only saying that he scared them off with the pickup truck. He said he didn't report it because he had no evidence, no plate number and no witnesses. The detective, a man named Eli Forde, didn't appear to have believed a word that James had said but took notes.

A different detective, a woman named Mila something-he-couldn't-pronounce, returned on day three and spoke to Lauren, who gave her a recap and a description of the shooter; a little taller than her so 5'7" or 5'8", thin with ropey muscles like a rock climber, brown hair. 'He looks like Ed Harris from...' she pauses.

Detective Mila: 'State of Grace?'

James: 'Who?'

Tori: 'The Abyss.'

Nurse in the room checking Lauren's IV: 'Enemy at the Gates.'

A man named Kenneth from the security company is in the room with them, looking more like Secret Service than private security; a tall black man with a neat beard and a well-fitted suit.

He and Detective Mila seem to know each other in a slightly awkward way.

Kenneth says, 'Robocop.'

James: 'Aaah.'

Lauren: 'I was going to say 'Gravity' but yeah, like that, with hair. Mid 30s Ed Harris.'

Detective Mila: 'Like Scott Eastwood?'

James: 'Who?'

Nurse: 'Now that would be a step up in my book.'

Tori, to James: 'Clint Eastwood's son.'

Lauren: 'No, he's too good looking. This guy was more plain than that.'

Security Kenneth: 'Like how Edward Burns is a plainer Billy Baldwin?'

Nurse, dreamily: 'Billy Baldwin.'

Lauren, Googling Edward Burns: 'Exactly!'

Detective Mila: 'And he just walked off and got in his car?'

Lauren: 'Yes, a red Hyundai. I remember seeing the slanty H symbol on the trunk.'

Detective Mila: 'And you have no idea why him or anyone would want to kidnap you or hurt you?'

Lauren: 'I think I surprised him by reaching in my bag. Maybe he was trying to get me to go along with him but thought I had a gun. No. We thought it might be this guy Chance Baris but we have no proof of that at all.'

Nurse: 'Chance Baris from 'Wild and Young?'

An eyebrow raised from Mila.

Kenneth: 'He's pretty rich. Made money in tech before getting into movies.'

Nurse skeptically mumbles 'Hm' and leaves.

Lauren: 'He owns a nightclub. He hit on me a few times and I got a bad feeling from him but that was all.'

Mila: 'When was the last time you saw him?'

Lauren: 'About a month ago? My friend Molly likes to go to his club, the Blue Katana.'

Mila: 'What about you, ma'am?' she says to Tori. 'Anyone who would want to hurt you through your daughter?'

Tori: 'I help find funding for medical scholarships that benefit underprivileged students.'

Mila looks at her flatly, her eyes saying that is not what I asked you but understanding Tori's point just the same. 'James?'

James says, 'I hadn't met her before the attempted kidnapping.'

She thinks and no one speaks for about twenty seconds, her jaw making a weird movement while she does it. ‘Ok, where will you be staying when you leave?’

James: ‘My place. 430 Palm Drive in Hermosa Beach.’

Mila hands Lauren a card. ‘Be careful. Keep someone with you at all times, if possible. They made it seem like you died with putting the room under a different name and all but someone might see you. I’m going to work on this and will have questions so all of you should put my number into your phone so you don’t send me to voicemail,’ putting emphasis on the ‘send me to voicemail’ part.

She continues, ‘and if you think of anything, shoot me an email. I will talk to you if you call but can organize everything better if it is in an email.’

‘Oh!’ Lauren says, ‘I got distracted by Ed Harris and almost forgot. He was wearing glasses and scrubs but I think the glasses were fake. Not good fakes either, like old fake ones with gold metal rims.’

‘Ed Harris was pretty distracting’, Kenneth said, and Tori nodded to him with a look that said, ‘fair enough’.

‘That’s good,’ Mila said to Lauren, ‘keep doing that. Keep thinking of things. If we don’t get someone right away, the small things catch up to them.’

-

“Harriett” is discharged on day six. Lauren has been walking the halls of the hospital but slowly, trying not to open a wound but trying to get her recovery going. The stairs at James’ will not be happening on the first day. Lauren is daunted by the stairs and also very upset that she is. It’s just stairs. But she is still shuffling and won’t be able to get her feet up high enough to take the risers. She also doesn’t want to feel trapped on the second floor so tells James that the first floor will do.

In low Ugg boots, gray Puma sweatpants and a matching gray Puma sweatshirt over a tee and a bra that James picked up for her, Lauren is comfortable on the outside. She is not very comfortable on the inside yet and is worried about weaning off the medication. 'Get through today,' she thinks.

James: 'I have to believe that whoever shot you followed us to or from Hermosa Beach. So I have an alternate solution, if you are okay with it.'

Lauren: 'Shopping cart in a doorway in Malibu?'

James: 'Santa Monica. We can lay low there.'

James and Kenneth the security guy walk with Lauren, who is in a wheelchair being pushed along by (according to her name tag) Crystyl, a transportation orderly, down an elevator to a side exit and a waiting white minivan. Kenneth is talking to unseen people in what could be code but sounds like gibberish. Without turning too much, Lauren asks James, 'Is Ken okay?'

James replies, 'He's just planning the counter-surveillance.'

'The what?', Lauren asks, but they arrive at the minivan and they go through the procedure of getting Lauren out of the chair and in the sliding side door.

When she is in, she looks back to thank Crystyl and Kenneth but Kenneth is magically not there.

They talk on the ride about pain levels, medication and physical therapy. When they arrive in Santa Monica, there is only a wooden garage door in a stacked stone wall that looks like it is part of the mountain. James hits a button on a clicker and the door goes up quickly.

Inside the underground garage is enough space for at least 8 cars, Lauren thinks, and almost all of the spots are empty. There is a low-roof, 10' trailer with plain white walls against one side, its little wheel lowered to hold up the side that you tow it from. It resembles a typical underground condo lot but it has a work bench of some sort near the elevator.

They ride up to two, coming out of the elevator between a living room and a dining room, each the size of her apartment but with high ceilings. Past the dining room sits a new stone floor kitchen with seemingly a hundred cabinets and a refrigerator that looks like the doors are made from TV panels. The largest exterior wall housed wood and glass bi-fold doors that are currently folded open to reveal a thirty-five hundred square foot deck, with grass, palm trees and a massive pool. Beyond and below the stacked stone wall is the Pacific Ocean.

Lauren, moving slowly, one hand subconsciously near her stomach, says to James sardonically, 'I can see how someone would consider this 'laying low''. Before he can reply, his phone vibrates and he answers it on a tiny earbud she hadn't seen before.

James says, 'Hey', then 'okay thanks' and touches the earbud once to end the call. 'Sorry about that,' he says, 'that was Kenneth. He says we're clean.'

'I somehow lost him in the hospital. He was walking with us and then just not there. And I'm observant,' Lauren says.

'That was pretty good. He went to get his car moving to run the counter-surveillance. He checked the place out and approved it when I told him about it. Said it is very defensible but I don't think a war is going to break out here.'

Lauren asks, 'I didn't know there were mountains in Santa Monica. Is this another project?'

'Technically this is Pacific Palisades and yes, it is almost complete.' James replies.

'You're going to sell this?' What is this, $50 million?'

'Twenty-nine. I didn't buy it outright. I used other assets as the down payment and only pay the monthly mortgage for a few months while we updated it. And someone is already buying it, which is a relief since houses like this usually take a long time to sell.'

'I spoke to my friend Molly while I was in the hospital and she wants to come meet you. I think she believes that I made you up. That maybe I have had a psychological break or something.'

'This place is still a little dusty, no artwork or anything if you are okay bringing her here. I can ask Kenneth to pick her up.'

Lauren looked incredulous. 'We will probably have to take her out somewhere. This place is,' and she mimed putting her finger down her throat in a gag. The place was magazine-cover beautiful.

'Embarrassing,' James said, looking across the pool at the yard and shaking his head. 'The lounge chairs haven't even come in yet.'

Lauren wasn't sure if he was serious or not but moved on. They had a playful banter and it had a rhythm to it. 'Maybe you can pick her up in the minivan.'

'Is she into that?' James asked.

'Duh. Who isn't? Oh, and whatever you do, don't tell her my heritage. She has been guessing for years and I never give her an answer.'

James called Kenneth to say he will pick up Molly, but Kenneth asked for the address. Lauren called Molly and said someone would come pick her up, only saying that he looked like a young Jerry Rice. She'd text when he was there. Molly replied, 'Delicious' and hung up.

They went back inside and sat at the kitchen island on barstools. Lauren was a little worried that she wouldn't be able to get up from the couch by herself or that it would hurt.

James got two waters from one of the side-by-side TV screens that were actually refrigerator doors and sat beside Lauren at the island. She was thinking. 'I think I'm missing something important.'

-

Molly came in wearing cream colored platform (wicker? James didn't know) shoes, a white miniskirt that was almost a belt, skin colored halter top that made you look twice and white crop top jean jacket. She looked like LA Summer Barbie. Her hair was several different well-blended shades of blonde and brown, her eyes hidden behind large Christian Dior sunglasses. A small bag dangled absently from an arm.

She went straight for Lauren and hugged her shoulders gently, making sure not to hurt her. 'Are you okay?' she asked, looking serious over her lowered Diors to look Lauren in the eyes. She rolled her eyes to the left quickly to indicate James and barely audibly said, 'He good?'

Lauren smiled and nodded.

James, to Molly: 'Can I get you something to drink?'

'A Lemon Drop Martini or a Moscow Mule would work,' she said, setting down her tiny bag on the kitchen counter

‘That’ll take a little bit but I can give you a water in the meantime,’ James replied. He went to the TV-looking fridge and pulled out a bottle of water. ‘I have to order the ingredients.’

‘Awesome,’ said Molly, slowly looking James up and down. Then to Lauren, ‘I call Little Sister.’

Lauren stifled a laugh and held her belly.

‘What is that?’ James asked, wanting to be in on the joke.

Lauren, still giggling but trying not to, finally said, ‘She is putting in the claim for the hand-me-down.’

Molly puts her sunglasses on the counter and elaborates. ‘You know, when she grows out of you or she doesn’t like you anymore, I get to wear you for a little while. Like, when you are out of style.’

James, looking shocked, mouth open. He takes a beat and says, ‘That’s terrible! But I’m in,’ he adds quickly, his horrified look shifting to a smile in an instant.

Lauren said, ‘That was too fast. You guys are making me nervous.’

James thought about it and said, ‘That’s only for when you are done with me. Right Molly?’

Molly, looking over James again: ‘Uh huh. Suuure.’ A smile, teasing Lauren. And Lauren knew it.

‘You two are not allowed in the hot tub together. Because I can’t go in for a while,’ she looked down at her bandaged stomach.

‘Poor Boo,’ Molly said. ‘Tell me what is going on.’

-

Lauren began with the attempted kidnapping, James jumping in when he hit the van with the pickup truck. Lauren told about the getaway, the two weeks in Hermosa and then being shot by a child actor or someone like that.

They talked with each other seamlessly, sharing the story, as Molly looked back and forth tennis-style while they spoke. It looked as if they had rehearsed it. They had repeated it a few times by this point to the police, to Edgar, Kenneth and to Lauren’s mom so they sort of had.

-

James thought about what to do next while Molly and Lauren caught up. Since the house was new, there was no food or plates, glasses or silverware. He ordered sandwiches, a Jamba Juice for Lauren, alcohol, mixers, wine and beer to the house using Door Dash, texting Kenneth to let him know.

They did have enough furniture in the bedrooms if everyone wanted to sleep over, thankfully.

He obviously couldn't just wait for something else to happen to Lauren again so he would have to do something proactive about what was going on. He would see what he could find out. The police were looking for someone to arrest, not looking to go undercover or anything. First, he would have a private investigator look into Chance and the Blue Banana. He started Googling private investigators but texted Kenneth and asked if he had one. He said he didn't so he let Kenneth know about the Door Dash order. Googling for PIs it is.

He called one with good reviews and left a generic voicemail. He sent a second one a generic email.

The plan will be to look into it initially. Come up with some facts or good information for the police and hand it off. Get the ball rolling for them.

This, of course, is a terrible idea. James has no idea what to do in this situation but he doesn't see any other way. He could find someone to hire that will do this 'undercover' work for him but doesn't know if that is really a thing. He'll have the investigator look into the backgrounds of people from the club.

-

While James planned, Lauren and Molly talked about the temporary living conditions, who owned this house, where James had come from and are there more, work, sex and hair, in no particular order. James looked up on occasion and thought it was good to see Lauren not being serious. He thought she seemed serious too often. It was nice to see her be a girl.

-

Due to the sad lack of patio chairs, they hung out in the kitchen and living room (if that is what rich people called this place with sofas, TV and a giant wet bar), mostly telling funny stories from Molly and Lauren's adventures. Molly pushed Lauren into telling a few awkward stories that she hadn't shared before with James, with James listening and encouraging her to continue. They ate, Molly made a few delicious cocktails and they laughed. Kenneth joined them when the food came and told hilarious stories of celebrity 'Don't you know who I am' events that he had witnessed first-hand.

Edgar arrived unannounced in cargo shorts and a Fender t-shirt, seemingly to appear in the living room as if he had been there all along. James didn't say anything about his arrival or if he had been there the whole time, just including him in the conversation when he was there. Lauren noted that for later. How did he get there? Did Kenneth bring him as he had everyone else?

Molly made Edgar a Long Island Iced Tea, which he drank shockingly fast. He told a matter-of-fact story about accidentally melting the family sofa testing out a heat-transfer theory when he was 11. His dry delivery about his parent's reaction killed. He excused himself to go work on something, mumbling something that sounded like 'scooters'.

Molly, to James when Edgar left: 'How do you know him?'

James, acting as if Edgar was never there: 'Know who?'

Lauren, not drinking, took pain and anti-inflammatory medications at 4:30 as instructed, which made her sleepy. James took her up in the elevator to the bedrooms for a nap, bringing her to the double door master suite. She insisted that she just needed an hour or so and told him to keep Molly entertained outside of the hot tub. She has missed her friend and was truly enjoying her company. James told her to text him when she woke up so that he could help her sit up. He didn't want her to strain herself, and she agreed.

James and Molly had more drinks and more serious conversations while Lauren napped. This was good for Molly since she wanted to learn more about this mysterious guy who rides in on his orange horse and saves women from kidnapping. It wasn't that she didn't trust him, exactly, but had never met anyone like that. He sounded too good to be true, which might be the case.

Molly talked about her childhood, telling of her very pretty 'actress-socialite' mother and hard-working dad. How her mom never landed any decent parts and how her dad tried unsuccessfully to keep her mom happy. How she loved her mom but how her mom didn't pay attention to her very much when other people were around, always playing entertainer to anyone that came around. They became friends when Molly turned 18 and have stayed that way, which was fine.

James talked about his childhood, growing up in LA and then moving to the San Fernando Valley when he was in high school. He talked about how he started work right away when his parents died and went to school at the same time and how he didn't have much of a social life since.

Molly made another round of drinks and made another Long Island Iced Tea for Edgar, who didn't seem to be there. She left it on the end of the bar for him and they retreated back into the kitchen.

The conversation turned back to Molly, who tried to gloss over her college experience, but James stopped her to ask what she studied.

'It's stupid,' she replied.

'Was it Philosophy? Religious Studies?' James asked.

'No, and no. Archaeology and Art History,' Molly said, head lowered in shame.

James' mouth dropped open. 'You hate money,' he said and pointed, smiling. 'I'm kidding. Those are great majors, if you like learning and teaching. Nothing wrong with that.'

'Thanks,' Molly said, smiling, and liking James a little more.

'Where did you go?'

'Oregon,' she said. 'You?'

'Pepperdine,' he said, almost embarrassed. 'It's close.'

'You're apologizing for going to Pepperdine? Weeirdooo!' Molly said, the last word in a sing-song voice.

James asked, 'So here is the question I have been waiting to ask. Who do you think would do something like this to Lauren? Is it this Chance guy?'

'Let me explain Chance, or at least how I see him. He gives me the creepy vibe but not more than other dudes from other countries. Like French guys or Italian guys, off the boat. Not Americanized ones. They're all about you when they want to get in your pants and treat you like the hottest girl in the world but won't look at you again after they get it.' She explained. 'Like Eastern European guys, which I think he is.'

'But,' she continued, 'maybe he was a bit more than that with Lauren. I don't know because I would usually be off dancing or talking to other guys that don't give me that vibe and not listening in on their 'conversations'', she said with air quotes. 'I think mostly he was laying down the rap though. He tried a little with me when Lauren rejected him but he always liked her. Maybe it's the smart thing or the hard-to-get thing. Weird because he's good looking, rich, owns a night club, which is cool, and works in movies, which is cool. He can get tons of girls. And does, from what I can tell.'

James said, 'You see him going home with them?'

'Well, we never stay that late at the club but there is a bartender that I talk to sometimes that sorta said he gets a lot. That's another thing. So chatting up girls real close is a little creepy, we all get that. But why is a guy who slept with a lot of women gross? I think it is the *intention*.' James turned his head to the side when she said that, like a puppy. 'I'll explain.'

'Say I'm out at the Katana or at a place on the strip and hanging with a rando, you know, random dude. Most guys are pretty cool about it. You give out your number or hook up with someone, it's fun. Everybody knows what it is. If someone stays overnight, you are only obligated to see if they have a way home. Maybe you text. Sometimes you like him or he likes you and you date but, if not, no biggie. There's no *objective*. Chance, or dudes who sleep with *too* many women, seem to have a weird mission or something. That is the part I don't trust.'

'Sounds like you really thought about this,' James said.

'Not really. I can't explain it. There are some things in life that are just what they are. Lauren would tell me that my 'preconceived notions about men from other countries is probably a product of movies or the media' or some BS, but it's not. She would be right to say that they are my biases based on my experiences.'

'You're right. Sometimes you just know things. Like, for example, I just know that Edgar's drink is empty without turning around.'

They looked over to the end of the bar and saw that the drink that Molly had left for him was, in fact, empty.

'Weeirdooos,' Molly said in the sing-song voice again, a little softer this time, putting on a worried expression for comedic purposes, which got a laugh out of James.

James' pocket vibrated with an incoming text. Checking his watch, he said, 'Lauren's up.' Molly started to volunteer to get her up but James was already heading for the stairs.

Molly thought, man, he's fast.

-

After some hair and teeth brushing, James brought the sweatpanted Lauren down in the elevator and they made their way slowly back to the kitchen. When they arrived, Lauren had an announcement.

'I remembered something,' she said as she tried to look casual partially sitting on a bar stool.

James and Molly looked on, not saying anything.

'The shooter was on like 2 episodes of 'Scrubs' and in that cop movie with Ethan Hawke. He was the younger partner who gets killed by the gang like halfway through. Christopher Scott Williams I think.'

Molly already had her phone out and was on IMDB. 'Christopher William Scott,' she pronounced ten seconds later. She turned her phone around to show a head shot of the actor.

'Yeah, that's him, without the glasses. Kinda short?'

Molly: '5' 8" it says, but that is usually an inch or two off. It says Tom Cruise is 5' 8" also. Good thing it only measures height,' she added. 'I've seen Chance talking to him at the Katana. I'm pretty sure he's a regular there.'

Lauren was wearing a far-away look when she said, 'I think I remember him being there on St. Patrick's Day. Molly, can you pull up your pictures from March?'

Molly did. She was always taking selfies and group pictures wherever they went. She shared pictures directly with people all the time but only shared pictures on social media with permission from everyone in the shot, and even then, not often. She rarely jumped into a group shot someone she didn't know was capturing.

Despite James' earlier thinking, Lauren did have an Instagram account and a Facebook page. The Instagram was to relax her brain when she was mobile, watching random reels and checking in on friends. The Facebook was good for catching up with family, younger and older.

Molly came up with 15 pictures from the inside of an Irish pub and 6 pictures from the Katana on St. Patrick's Day. The pub shots were mostly pictures of Molly with one other person seated at a bar in a green shirt, green sparkly hat and/or green sunglasses. Molly looked to be invading their personal space but everyone was smiling, some with mugs of green beer, some with amber-colored beer. One was of Lauren with a man and a woman near a dart board, hamming it up for the shot, wearing green shirts and beads.

The Katana pictures were of people dressed up a little nicer, no green beer-related t-shirts here. There were girls in bikinis and high heels doing promotional drink specials for an Irish whiskey in one shot, one of Molly and Lauren at a table, the left side of Molly's face up against Lauren's right, Chance talking to Christopher William Scott near the bar in the background.

All three leaned in to see the picture and Molly resized it on the screen, zooming in on the pair. 'Damn, there's your evidence,' said James, excited by the finding. 'Send that to me.'

'It's not exactly evidence but it does establish that they know each other,' Lauren added, bringing the excitement down a little.

'I wonder if the bouncer was that huge dude who grabbed me?' Lauren pondered.

Molly asked, 'What did he look like?'

Lauren replied, 'Tall, gym-muscular, dark brown or black hair, brown eyes, square jaw. He looked Italian.'

Molly was nodding by the time she got to 'black hair.' 'Tony,' she said the second Lauren stopped talking. 'Kinda good looking but Neanderthal-ish?'

'Yep. He was in the doorway of the van when James hit it.'

'Ouch.' Molly said, wincing.

'It didn't look good for him. Hey, why didn't we see if he was at West Hills after the accident?' James asked rhetorically.

'I guess because we're not cops?' Lauren asked, palms up near her shoulders. She genuinely never thought of that.

'I don't have any pictures of Tony but he worked there sometimes. Maybe like only on Thursdays or something so we didn't see him too often. I talked to him once or twice. He seemed nice enough but looked a little menacing. Small forehead.'

'He definitely looked menacing when he was trying to drag me into the van,' Lauren added.

'To recap, we're assuming that Chance, who is rich and not ugly, hires a D-list actor and a bouncer to kidnap our little Lauren, a cute and possibly part Asian Nerdoscientist, off of the street in broad daylight,' Molly says, vocalizing what everyone is alluding to. 'How hard was he trying with you because that seems over-the-top extra.'

Lauren contemplated for five seconds. 'Reasonably hard. But I feel like if someone was at the kidnapping stage, they would have tried a lot harder. Like holding-up-a-boombox-outside-your-house hard. Or boiling-your-bunny-rabbit hard.'

Molly didn't get the bunny rabbit reference and James didn't get the boombox reference but they did get the general idea though. Lauren saw their faces and added, 'I watched way too many movies with my mom as a kid when my dad was traveling.'

'Was he traveling to the Philippines at all?' Molly asked.

Both Lauren and James ignored the Asian comments from Molly, who said, 'Really? Nothing?'

Satisfied that they had solved part of the mystery, James, Lauren and Molly talked for another three hours, with their feet in the jacuzzi or laying out on the semi-circular couches, when they all decided to go to sleep.

They called the never-sleeping Kenneth, who alertly said 'Copy that.'

-

They slept upstairs, James and Lauren in the master bedroom, Molly in a room across the hall with an en-suite bathroom. They met on the semi-circular couches around 8AM, and since James forgot to buy coffee or a coffee maker, went to early breakfast at the Playboy diner in Santa Monica, a Sixties-themed restaurant, Kenneth joining their group. Molly never noticed the rest of the security team but James and Lauren thought they did, noting at least three serious-looking people in rotation on foot and in cars going around the diner.

Tori met them at the Playboy with her bag in her car. She was excited to stay at the Santa Monica house, finding out what it looked like from Lauren. Lauren didn't send pictures, as Kenneth had instructed.

-

Billy calls Chance to tell him about the pickup gone wrong. 'She reached into her bag when she saw me. She probably had a gun,' Billy says. Chance throws a fit, screaming and cursing on the other end of the phone but Billy stays quiet.

'It's not your fault,' Chance finally says after a few minutes. 'It's not your fault. You should have shot her in that situation.'

11.

Misty McCarthy was a bartender at the Blue Katana. No one knows for how long, not even Chance. Two years maybe? Large brown eyes, sandy blond and quiet, with a small nose and wide lips, very attractive in an innocent way. Most folks make the mistake of thinking that Misty is stupid. The revealing clothes they make the girls wear at the Katana did nothing to help the image but they definitely helped the tips.

Misty was far from stupid.

She moved from Fresno to LA, hoping to act long enough to make money for school and a modest house for her and her brother. She knew most actresses had a shelf life and that hers would be short. Her look was impossible to change so she would most likely be typecast, which is fine for a while.

Her real motivation was her brother Jake.

-

Her mother was a scientist who worked at a lab in a semi-unpopulated area north of Fresno. Her father was a smart, blue-collar guy who built store fronts.

Her childhood was wonderful. Her parents were both fun, concentrating their energy after work on her and her brother. They watched movies, played board games and every Friday one of the four would make up a game and they would all play it. Once someone made up a new version of hide-and-seek, once it was Socialist Monopoly, once it was Uno in Reverse so that the reverse card was forward and where you wanted someone else to win. They did homework together. They always ate dinner at the dining room table together. Until Misty turned nine.

Her mother, Rena, received a promotion at work, taking her supervisor's place when he retired. They went on vacation that summer to Hawaii, a first for their small clan. Traditionally they would find campsites or small cabins to visit in the summers, which were fun and allowed them to keep the kids in private schools during the year. 'Education is more important than vacation,' her mom would say.

The downside was that now she worked all the time. Her father Ted McCarthy tried carrying on with the traditions, dinner at the table, games with the kids, but it was tiring and he slowly and illogically grew bitter toward their mom. Mom would get home from work at 9 or 10pm, kiss her children and go straight to bed.

Ted started going out on Friday nights, leaving her and Jake who was thirteen at the time, alone to order food, with Jake trying to entertain Misty. He would use the oven mitts as hand puppets, mute movies and make up ridiculous dialogue for the characters, anything to get her to smile. These things were childish for the unnervingly smart eleven-year-old Misty but she loved it. She grew closer to Jake during that time than she had before. Dad's friends grew rougher as he grew lonelier, dabbling in drugs now and again, coming home later and less often. Rena was so tired that she didn't know what to do about it.

By the time Misty was fifteen and Jake was seventeen, Jake rarely came home. Jake had a girlfriend that Misty did not like and they would drink a lot, even during the week. Their mom had thrown their dad out one night when he drove home completely drunk and smelling like a 'cheap whore', according to her mother. When that happened, she told the lab that she was now a single parent and needed to be home more often and they reluctantly complied.

Mom started dating, stating that Ted had not been around for going on three years. It was awkward for her and Jake, but mostly for her. And while her mom was very book smart, she wasn't a great judge of character. Mom never let anyone sleep over and would make sure Jake was home (yeah, right) if she was going to sleep out.

That was when it happened. The event that changed her life.

She realized at that point that her family wasn't coming back and made a plan to get the hell out of Fresno.

After finishing high school at eighteen, she got a real-but-fake driver's license from a meth head who worked at the central Fresno DMV. All of the information was correct, but he had changed her birthdate by three years. She headed to LA in her hand-me-down car with whatever money she could scrape together from mom and dad. She needed money to help get Jake away from Fresno and from the drug problem that was eating Fresno like a cancer.

Billy was not doing well. He shot that girl twice (he thinks) but he didn't think she died. He didn't know why he thought it but he thought it anyway. Maybe he shouldn't have shot her in a hospital parking lot.

He was nervous about getting tracked down but also guilty about shooting her.

He was at the club late on Saturday night, drinking shots at the bar with Misty. He liked Misty even though she wouldn't date him. He had asked but she didn't seem to date. Hell, she didn't even seem to like anyone but they were somewhat friendly. And he really needed to talk to someone. She was like a sphinx; she wouldn't tell anyone anything.

Misty filled her shot glasses with water poured from a Chopin vodka bottle, the original contents poured out long ago. She was not stupid enough to drink with the customers who insisted that she drink with them. They usually drank Don Julio tequila or Grey Goose vodka or Jack Daniels. She drank water from the Chopin bottle alone and no one noticed that she never got drunk.

Billy was talking about a problem he helped Chance with that he thought Chance should give him a lot of money for. Misty listened and processed information as it was given. She asked questions. Billy was very drunk. She let him stay after the bar closed as she cleaned up and counted out, telling him no more drinking, but gave him a Coors Light to maintain his buzz and encouraged him to keep talking. She was a friend after all.

Misty had a good idea about what had happened by 2:20am but wanted Billy to keep talking.

Billy got up to use the bathroom while Misty was putting away glasses. About 15 minutes when by when she realized he'd been gone too long. She went out from behind the bar and down to the bathrooms but didn't find Billy. He must have ducked out the back door and drove in his completely drunken state. Man, was that stupid.

While she was in the back, she went to the office and pulled up the cameras on the desktop computer. Most of the staff had access to the cameras so that if there was a problem and Chance was on a set, they could pull up footage for the police.

She found Camera Seven, the closest camera to her end of the bar, and copied the footage from 12:10am to 2:30am. She logged into her cloud storage and copied the footage, which took nine minutes. She logged out of her cloud storage, erased the camera storage and locked the computer.

12.

James gets a call back from one of the investigators, a woman named Willie Bard (short for Wilamena? He didn't know), who said she was happy to discreetly look into Chance Baris and Christopher William Scott. She notes that her investigation would not be tainted by whatever is in the press, since most of that was made up nowadays. James could Google that if he wanted to. She would see what she could find out and they would discuss the next steps afterward.

James didn't think that anyone would go to the Blue Katana to snoop, not the police nor the investigator. After hearing Molly explain it, the idea that Chance orchestrated everything did sound pretty far-fetched. He knew it was true or at least partly but realized that no one else would really believe it.

James had found out from Molly who the bartender was in the picture with Chance and Billy. A girl named Misty, she said, who seemed very deer-in-the-headlights to Molly but was behind the bar every time she went. She would know something. He decides that it is worth checking out. Maybe this Misty isn't so bright and he can get information from her.

-

Phyllis had been working at the hospital for almost 20 years before meeting Lauren at lunch one day. There weren't too many people eating in the lunchroom post-Covid and they saw each other regularly. They started eating together and became friends. Phyllis, a married forty-eight-year-old customer service specialist with three kids, and Lauren, a twenty-eight-year-old shy Neuroscientist, seemed like unlikely friends but they talked most days whether it was in the lunchroom, by text or even by phone, if on had something interesting or funny to bring up.

Their friendship had a slight mother-daughter quality to it since Phyllis was quite a bit older. She would give advice, which Lauren gladly accepted, but most of their time was spent laughing. Sometimes they laughed at Phyllis' kids or husband, sometimes it was Lauren's social life, but they laughed a lot.

Their favorite subject was Phyllis' husband Walter. Phyllis and Walter had 3 girls who were currently ages sixteen, fourteen and twelve. Walter absolutely never gets what he wants (or needs, for the most part) and sometimes jokingly complains about it but loves his girls and his life. When at work, Phyllis says 'poor Walter' a lot to friends like Lauren but never lets Walter know that she feels bad for him. 'If I sympathize with him once, he'll use that like a crowbar on me until the end of time. We can't have *that*.'

Phyllis is on at the hospital Monday morning when a call gets passed to her from someone looking for Lauren. She sounds like a nice young kid, like Lauren, but Phyllis is suspicious.

-

'Hi,' the caller said in a nice, but authoritative, tone, 'I'm looking for a fellow doctor that I was sharing research with, Lauren Parker? I sent her over an email with some research data from a project that we are working on here at Oak Hills and I got a bounceback. I have her email, lauren.parker at westhillsmed.com and I've emailed and talked to her before so it's weird to have her phone go straight to voicemail and her email not work. I want to ask if she's okay but understand if you can't tell me. People leave jobs all the time but we talked a lot. I liked her.'

'I can probably find her on LinkedIn. Is there someone else in her department that I can forward the data to? Or an alias, like 'neuroscience at westhillsmed'? I'd hate for their project to stall.'

The confirmation of Lauren's email address lowered Phyllis' guard a little. That and the fact that the caller moved on to sharing the research pretty quickly instead of pressing harder.

'May I ask who is calling?' Phyllis asked.

The caller said they were from the Oak Hills Research Center. Oak Hills was a real place and Phyllis looked online while the caller was speaking.

Since she had passed a lot of people over to him recently, she had Dr. Pearson's info memorized and was looking up Oak Hills on Google. 'Let me look up the contact information for you,' she said.

'You can send the research to Lucas dot Pearson at westhillsmed dot com,' she said to the caller, and added, 'Lauren will be back in about six weeks. Thank you.'

She heard the caller say, 'Great. Thank you.' and hang up.

Phyllis ends the call with the feeling that she did something helpful. The nice person on the phone sounded worried. She'll text Lauren and let her know people cared for her. She takes her phone out to text when she gets a message from her eldest daughter. It is screamy in the way that only sixteen-year-old girls can be. She's in a rage because she just saw a picture of her younger sister, Margaret, wearing her favorite hoodie on Instagram, which was apparently 'not authorized.' She takes a deep breath, lets it out, and starts her reply, forgetting about the nice doctor for now.

13.

James calls the detective, Mila Something-he-couldn't-pronounce (her business card said Briçianos), on speakerphone and tells her that Lauren is seventy-five percent sure that the person who shot her was an actor named Christopher William Scott.

'From 'The Day After Tomorrow?' Mila asks.

'Inception,' says a pajama-clad Lauren.

'Ah. He fits the description that you gave me at the hospital. Seventy-five percent?'

'Probably more like eighty-five but I'm lowballing it,' Lauren replies. 'I don't remember seeing him in real life before the shooting and he wasn't exactly memorable in that movie. I had to IMDB him.'

'Okay thanks for that. We'll look into it,' Mila says and clicks off.

'Is she going to do anything?' Lauren asks.

'If she is, she isn't going to tell us about it.' James says. He goes on to tell Lauren and Tori about his plan to go to the club and ask some questions.

'That doesn't seem smart,' Tori, shoeless, dressed in flowy linen pants and a matching shirt, says from the kitchen table without looking up from her iPad.

'It's not smart at all. Let's let the police handle it,' Lauren says from her spot on the couch. She's getting up and down a little better today but James goes and helps her whenever she wants to move.

'I hired an investigator over the weekend to look into Chance and this guy. She's doing background on them but won't go undercover or anything. There's no proof and no cameras in the middle of the parking lot. Are they going to ask for confessions?' James said.

Lauren looked worried. 'I don't want you to get shot too. He might kill you and that wouldn't be fair to me. I'd have to leave this house,' she added at the end to keep things light.

'Ok, I'll be careful. If I think for a second there is going to be trouble, I'll call the police. I just don't want to hang around waiting for whoever shot you to find us.'

Tori, still not looking up from her iPad added in a dry, casual voice, 'Maybe you should put this house in our names just in case there is an emergency...'

-

James, dressed in gray jeans, black hi-tops and a black t-shirt, goes from the Santa Monica house to his house in Hermosa Beach to pick up a different car. He returned the minivan on Sunday, brought his parents' Mercedes back to the Granada Hills house and brought the pickup to the mechanic before the shooting. That left the Rivian and the Aston Martin. The Rivian was one of a million in LA but not with the solar panels built into the sunroof. The Aston was not very stealthy as cars went but it would do if he needed to leave quickly.

He'd thought about getting another car but had four cars at the moment, so maybe not. Lauren's car might already be known so he didn't use that.

He bought a burner phone with cash (he reads books) at the mall and felt ridiculous. He was carrying three phones right now. His personal phone, his business phone and the burner. He memorized the number of the burner after he bought it. He felt like a terrible spy.

He parked in the parking lot on the side of the nightclub and looked around. There were a few cars in the lot but nothing that looked like it belonged to the owner, Chance. He would have something flashy. He set his work cell phone to record audio before heading to the front door of the club.

It was still early (8pm) and he was hoping that it wouldn't be too loud or too busy. From outside the door, the music sounded faint, which was a good sign. When he opened the door, the music was twice as loud but he wouldn't have to yell over it. He walked in and went to the end of the bar where there was a girl with her back to him. He hoped that it was Misty. Since the other bartender was male, this was the better odds.

She turned around and asked, 'What can I get you?'

James was ninety percent sure it was Misty, based on the picture Molly showed her, but would find out to be sure. She was pretty and had innocent, big eyes but there was something in them, some steel he thought. It wasn't her facial expression or her mannerisms.

Misty was short, 5'2" or 5'3", but had an air of authority about her, making her seem bigger. She smiled at him but it didn't reach her eyes, which shouldn't be unusual for a bartender in a nightclub. James thought she seemed like a police officer.

The black, low-cut top and tight jeans showed off her fit body, most likely for tips. Her arms weren't muscular but shapely, strong. She didn't have the larger lats or oversized trapezius of a gym rat though.

James didn't think she would dress like that outside of here but he didn't know her yet to be sure. She did seem confident enough to wear whatever she wanted.

'A bottle of Stella, if you have it,' James replies.

She nodded, walked three paces down the bar and opened an under-counter fridge. She bent, pulled out a Stella and a frosted pint glass, opened the Stella with a flat bottle opener she had barely room for in her back pocket and placed the bottle and glass on the bar in front of James. 'Seven.'

James gave her a ten and started to pour the beer into the cold mug. 'What time does this place pick up?' he asked.

'Well,' Misty started, 'you picked a great night. Tuesdays used to be Porn Star Karaoke night but Covid killed that. So for Tuesdays, there'll probably be ten or twelve people in here at the high point, around 10PM.' she said sarcastically. She picked up the ten, took three singles out of the register and James shook her off. She stood on her tiptoes to put them into a giant glass chalice that was taking up acreage behind the bar with the few other bills that were in there.

'Oh, actually that sounds good to me. I wanted to ask you a few questions if you don't mind....'

Misty leaned against the back bar and folded her arms as he said this, pushing her breasts up with her forearms. She was looking at him as if he were an idiot. She's not stupid, James thinks.

James says, 'I can make it worth your while.' Her eyebrows crinkled and she started to put up her hands in a stop gesture. 'Oh, wait, that sounded wrong. I wanted to ask about a guy named Christopher William Scott,' James got out before she called security.

Interesting, Misty thinks. 'You mean Billy,' she says. Not a question.

'If that is what you call him, yeah.'

'He comes in here sometimes. Actor,' Misty says.

James: 'Yep, that's him. Does he work here?'

Misty: 'Nope.'

James took a sip of his beer. 'He comes in here though?'

Misty took a quick look around. No one was paying attention to them. She looked at the bar and back up at James.

'I know him,' she says.

'Ok cool. I'm pretty sure he shot my friend and I don't know why. Or if he's going to do it again.' James noted that Misty did not look horrified to hear this and thought that maybe she knew quite a bit.

Misty: 'I'm not sure about that but I can find out. What is it you are really looking for? And what is your name?'

James: 'James. I'd like to know that, if he did do it, he's not going to follow us or shoot her again.'

Misty: 'I'm Misty. Let's say that he did shoot her, hypothetically. Do you want him to disappear?'

James: 'I'm not going to pay him to run away, no.'

While Misty assumed that this was her boyfriend, he did look like he could be a cop. She leveled a flat stare at James.

James paused for a minute, not getting it. Then the light bulb lit. 'Oh hell no. I'm not asking for anything illegal. I want to see him go away or go to jail.'

Misty: 'Ok good. I don't want you to think that I'm a contract killer or anything.' She smiled at him, this time it touched the corners of her eyes. 'What if I can get him to meet you. Maybe you could record the meeting and he would confess, or at least incriminate himself?'

James: 'That might work, if we meet in a place with a lot of people and cameras. I don't want him shooting me too.'

Misty: 'Let me see what I can do. No guarantees. I'll tell him you think it was him so maybe he'll talk.'

James: 'Thanks.' He took out the burner phone and unlocked it to get her number and Misty took it from him. She seemed to look around for a few seconds before entering her contact info into the phone. She put in her number and an 'M' for the name and called herself. When her phone vibrated in her back pocket, she hit 'end'.

She put the phone down on the bar and said, 'Let me see your real phone.'

James looked up as if he were going to play stupid but she was looking at him flatly again. He took out his personal phone and unlocked the screen. He opened the recent apps and she looked for something recording but didn't find anything. She clicked on his texts and saw a bunch without opening a specific one and then closed it, satisfied that it was not also a burner.

Misty said, 'I'll call you in a day or two. Don't hang out here too long, I don't want anyone putting this together later on.'

James said, 'Please be very careful. He was willing to shoot my friend and I don't want you to get hurt, too. And thank you for doing this.' He put his mostly empty beer down and left.

Misty's brain was moving, playing out all the different ways that this could happen.

She could tell Chance all of this. What would she do, blackmail her seemingly-shady boss who was most likely armed? That was punching above her weight class so she thought it through a few times.

When James left, Misty went out from behind the bar and looked out into the parking lot to see if she could nonchalantly catch James leaving. She pictured him as a pickup truck guy for some reason. He looked like he had money so it would be a nice truck, like a new GMC. But she was wrong. She watched as a silver Aston Martin Vantage rolled out of the parking lot and thought she should have asked for money.

She also thought he was hot. He wasn't pretty like a lot of LA guys but had a great body. Strong. He came in trying to protect his girlfriend and was worried that she, Misty, might get hurt too. So he's nice but is very strong and seems like he could hold me down and do whatever. Maybe in that Aston Martin. Hmm. Maybe ON that Aston Martin...

Misty didn't normally get turned on when she met guys. She liked guys but they usually were just *guys.* Like they were all a little doofy, watching sports and drinking beer like that was something to be excited about. And they dressed like crap, wearing cargo shorts and flip flops to a club. She didn't get it.

Girls were hotter physically and she had dated a few pretty ones. She dated a few guys too but none that went to a physical relationship since high school. She was smart and liked smart. She thought maybe she'd been working in a night club too long or maybe it was just LA, but it was hard to find smart people her age. Well, the age she was pretending to be.

But today, that might have changed. At least with James.

-

14.

A few days later, Chance arrived at the Blue Katana around ten. At around ten twenty, Misty goes to the back and knocks on his office door.

Chance and Misty had been 'friends' over the past two years. They'd started off as employer/employee in the beginning, talking strictly about bar business. Gradually they talked about patrons, making fun of the regulars, the strange ones, the hot ones.

After the first year, Misty started to attend the parties she was invited to. She was nervous that someone would find out her actual age, but the connections were important. She went to Hollywood after-parties, to friend's houses, to restaurant-bar industry parties.

She liked the latter the most. These were the no-nonsense people who waited tables for the don't-you-know-who-I-am crowd. They exchanged stories, they laughed about celebrity interactions, they were the real LA people.

As a club owner, Chance had been to a few of those parties. He'd shared stories of celebrities like everyone else, like making A-listers wait in line to get into the Katana behind Jules, who was a large trans bouncer at a dive bar in the valley. Or the funny story of him physically throwing out a stuntman twice his size that was close to punching someone but he didn't throw him through the window, which is where he thought stuntmen should be thrown.

Through all of that, Misty had never lied to Chance. The only time her drawer was low, she didn't outright blame the shifty-eyed druggie that Chance had hired. She told him relatable stories, which intersected with his ideals. Chance respected her. She seemed to be a straightforward person in this sea of transient leeches.

'Come in,' Chance says over the music. Misty, in black sneakers, a tight black skirt and black, low-cut top, pushed in the door and crossed the room. Chance was sitting behind his desk, computer off to one side. 'Have a seat.'

The 12 x 12 office housed a large wood table desk with a file cabinet on either side and two chairs in front, a sofa that Misty thought looked sticky even though it wasn't, a glass and gold-looking bar cart in the corner, a small private bathroom with the door closed on one side and sheetrock wall with a mirror and door to the parking lot on the other. Behind the desk was a concrete block wall with classic movie posters on it.

If I had money, I would make this nicer, Misty thinks to herself.

As she makes her way into a guest chair, Chance asked, 'What's up?'

Misty tells Chance that Billy got drunk a few days ago and was talking about a job he did for Chance that didn't go well. Something about a girl. While she told him that Billy didn't go into details, she could tell keeping the secret was bothering him.

She then tells him that a guy named James came in and asked if she knew a guy, 5'8", actor with a familiar face, etc. She said she told this James guy that she knew about ten people like that.

She said she thought to inform Chance since it didn't seem like a coincidence.

As Chance listens, standing, he thinks about Misty's motivation. Why is she here telling me this? She wants something, but what? He didn't know but everyone's motivations came out sooner or later. Since he 'trusted' her as much as he trusted anyone, he didn't push it.

"I'm not sure what Billy is really talking about but if you get accused of something, it would cost you a lot,' she finished.

He shrugged at that, telling Misty, 'Thanks for bringing that to me, I appreciate it. I don't know what Billy is talking about either but I'll ask him.'

Chance watched Misty's ass move in the skirt as she walked out, turned and sat heavily into his chair.

It didn't feel like she was blackmailing him but he thought he'd give her something for her loyalty. Everybody needed money. Maybe he could get her a part in something.

She's right though. It would cost him millions if this gets out. His friends, some of them being part of the Hollywood elite, would cast him out.

Acquaintances, he corrects. They are not friends. Chance spent his youth and adult life here and didn't think that unselfish friends really existed. That maybe they only existed in Hallmark movies and small towns. The people he called friends were cling-ons. It never crossed his mind that maybe he attracted those sorts of people because that is the way he was.

He would have to give Billy some money soon. It had been a while and, while he wasn't asking yet, he thought it would keep the wheels greased until something happened. He'd give him $5,000 to keep him happy. $5k was pocket money to Chance Baris.

Billy needs to keep his mouth shut. He doesn't want to give Misty up since confidential sources of information are always good, so he would act like he hadn't heard anything. He would just mention it in passing to keep his fucking mouth shut.

He realized that he lost track of Tony. He found out that Tony was (ironically) in Mission Hills Hospital after the crash and, if he said that he was working when it happened, that everything would be covered by Worker's Compensation. He had his assistant draw up paperwork and send it over.

His assistant, an efficient ex-production employee named Daniel, had moved to Columbus, Ohio, to take care of his dying mother. Chance still used him for stuff like paperwork and taxes. Danny seemed to be able to figure out everything and didn't ask a lot of questions, only the things he needed to know to accomplish a task.

So, where was Tony now? He sent him a text but didn't get a reply and there was no sign of him at West Hills Hospital.

-

James drove back to the Santa Monica house, running counter-surveillance the way that Kenny had taught him. He called Kenny on the way who told him someone would track him when he got close. He was thinking about Misty on the drive. Good-looking but hiding something? Probably not, he thinks, she just has to deal with the public on a daily basis. He thinks that but also thinks that he'll have to be careful with her.

14.

When James gets back to the Santa Monica house, he pulled into the underground garage through the high-speed roll up door and parked the Aston. On the way to the stairs, he paused to look at the steel-and-wire contraption on the workbench. He had absolutely no idea what it was but it looked like something from an Iron Man movie. He'd have to ask Edgar.

He found Lauren in the same place on the sofa reading a white paper on the Hippocampus or something, looking both smart and hot in her running shorts and tank top. Tori was no longer at the table. 'Where is your mom?', James asked.

'She just went upstairs to bed,' Lauren said, putting down her iPad. 'How did it go?'

'I met Misty. She seems okay but I don't think she trusts anyone. Like either she knows more than she's letting on or she called the cops on me when I left. I don't know her so maybe not. She is going to set up a meeting with me and Billy.'

'That doesn't seem like a good idea at all. I thought you were just going to find some stuff out.' Lauren was genuinely worried. 'He's not going to volunteer a bunch of information.'

'That's a good point. If I ask questions, he might just try and take me out,' James thought out loud. 'Ok, I'll stay away.'

Lauren paused. 'It can't be that easy. I express my concerns and you just AGREE? That's enough! Molly's right, you are hiding something! Where are the bodies buried, James? Is there a pile of dead girls in the back yard? Are you hiding a family somewhere?' She wasn't serious but a small part of her did feel like this relationship, like HE was too perfect.

James smiled and replied calmly, 'I think the problem is that I'm an adult. Most women our age are not used to dating adults so they look for the drama, thinking it is going to pop up like a jack-in-the-box and catch them by surprise. I will have to focus on work a little more here soon so everything doesn't fall apart but that's about it.'

'Of course you reply with simple logic,' Lauren says. 'I totally understand the situation but at the same time, I don't. There should be some kind of drama to a relationship.'

'Hmm,' James puts a hand on his chin in a thinking gesture. 'I'll have to think about that. I can bring up my ex-girlfriend sometimes if you think that will help.'

'Do not mock me, sir,' Lauren smiles slightly and wags a finger at him. His cologne still smelled wonderful.

'Pointing is rather rude. Maybe there should be some punishment involved.' James asked and shifted towards her on the couch.

'I think you're right...' Lauren said through her widening smile and adds, 'but be careful of the incisions...'

James scooped her up off of the couch and carried her towards the bedroom. 'I will do no such thing.'

As he carries her off the couch, through the bar, then dining room, up the stairs and down the hall, she starts to get heavy and he starts moving slower. He says, 'This isn't romantic anymore, is it.'

Lauren replies, 'It's just too far. I feel bad for you now.'

They both laugh when James croaks, 'I'm good' in a weak voice, puts her on the bed gently and falls down onto the floor next to it.

-

Misty sends Billy a text and says that she wants to talk to him about stuff, that she has some interesting details to share. Billy texted back, giving her his address. She texted back, '11:30?' and got an 'OK' back. Since the club was mostly empty, Mike, the other bartender, could close tonight on his own.

She thought there were a lot of different ways this could go. She'd bring her little can of mace if it went on the wrong side of things but she didn't think it would. Not that she had any experience doing something like this at all.

What was her end game? She thought about that, and her brother. Make money then get the hell out of here.

She counted out her drawer and collected half of the little cash from the monster tip jar, leaving the Blue Katana at 11pm. She drove an eleven-year-old silver Civic that her mom bought for her second hand, the odometer at 126,503 miles when it was new to her. It always started, it always ran. She had it for 3 years and added 60,120 miles to it and she doesn't remember even changing the battery. The paint was fading on the roof and the hood and the interior smelled like a wet dog, even though she didn't have a dog, but she thought the car would survive nuclear winter.

-

She arrived near Billy's address in Los Feliz at 11:20 and parked on the street. As is typical in Los Angeles, there were smaller houses running along the sides of a canyon next to larger houses, which were next to two-story mansions with big columns out front and expansive Italian villas. All of these lived on the same narrow street, which was barely wide enough for parked cars on one side and one car to go through at a time.

Billy's house was smaller and older looking than most of the others but not terrible. She thought maybe he bought it and didn't fix it like the neighbors did since single guys didn't necessarily fix up their houses like married guys do, but he probably just didn't have the money that the neighbors did.

The street was not particularly quiet for a Tuesday at 11:25pm. People were coming and going, lights were on everywhere in the houses and along the streets and hillsides. The freeway murmured in the background. She hoped that made her a little safer being alone with Billy but she didn't think so.

Misty arrived at his address and pushed the Ring. The bell made three sounds twice and Billy opened the door for her, grunted a salutation and walked back into the living room, leaving her to close the front door. Not the greeting she was hoping for. She was hoping for him to be a little more excited for her to be there but not overexcited. This was complete indifference.

Billy waved at some white couches and sat heavily into a low, white chair. The inside of the house was nicer than the outside. A blue and white Persian rug sat on old oak floor planks, white upholstered furniture sat on the rug and a few older-looking lamps stood in corners.

'What's going on?' He asked. He didn't offer a drink. His eyes looked tired, like he was going to bed soon.

She took a seat on one of the two sofas, keeping her legs close together. 'Lauren's boyfriend came by the bar. James. He was looking to find out if I knew you and if you worked there or something. I said you came in sometimes but I didn't know you. He asked for Christopher William Scott.'

Billy stopped moving, thinking about what this meant. If the police had evidence on him, they would have arrested him by now. He figured that Lauren recognized him in the parking lot from a movie. He must not be on camera anywhere then. After the pause, he asked, 'Does Chance know?'

Misty would have to be careful here. She didn't want Billy to know that she went to Chance but she liked that he was afraid of him. She would have to use it somehow.

'He saw him on the cameras but the sound was still off from the weekend.' Since the Katana was a night club, the music was very loud on the weekends and they turned off the sound recording. 'He asked me what he was doing there but I said just having a beer and making small talk. I don't know if he believed me or not but I think so.' She said this to get Billy to think she was colluding with him, that she was covering for him in some way.

Billy was nodding slightly but not talking. She realized that he hadn't said much and that she was doing all of the talking. Maybe he was recording this but, after processing that, realized it didn't matter to her. She couldn't incriminate herself or anything since she had no part in the shooting. So, might as well push on.

Misty said, 'James told me he wanted to meet you to ask you to back off. He said he doesn't want Lauren to get hurt again. He asked me to try and set up a meeting for 8pm next Tuesday at the club. I told him that if you came in that I would relay the message. He gave me a number but I think it was a pay-as-you-go phone. No contacts in it.' She thought it best not to call it a burner and make it sound like a spy movie.

Billy thought, I was right, Lauren is still alive. Fuck. He can't fix that now.

He looked at Misty for the first time since she had gotten there. He intentionally didn't look at her before because he wanted to hear what was happening without distraction. She was small-framed with big eyes and a young, innocent yet stern face, her low-cut, black lace top pushing her breasts up and together to defy the innocent face. Her sometimes-darker, sometimes-lighter hair fell around her shoulders in very large waves. Did she re-curl it before she came here?

Billy thought for the thousandth time that he would like to do her but wouldn't trust her enough to sleep next to her. He'd grown up on the streets back home and in Hollywood thought there was something not right with her. Like a water moccasin swimming just below the surface of a pristine lake. Pretty but dangerous. He thought about asking what her motivations were but knew she'd never tell him the truth. Being a guy, he figured he might as well try to get *something* from her.

After the second long pause, Billy asked, 'Do you want a drink? I'm shooting this week and don't normally drink when I'm working but could use one.' Misty was rapidly thinking about how to decline the drink but, in the interest of keeping up the camaraderie, said, 'Sure, I'll make us something.' She didn't trust him to make her a drink and wouldn't know what to do if he insisted on making her one but, thankfully, he stayed seated.

She stood and walked over to a tall wooden cabinet and swung open the double doors. A light came on and revealed an older, ornate bar with a few bottles and some short glasses.

Billy liked her getting up and making the drinks for them. It felt very 'Mad Men' to him.

Misty took out two rocks glasses and stepped into the nearby kitchen to get ice from a freezer door. She came back a few seconds later with two vodka and 7ups, handing one to Billy, who took it and she resumed her position on the couch. Without tinking glasses, he raised his glass, looked at her eyes and said, 'Cheers'. She mimicked his salute and took a tiny sip of the drink.

Drink in hand, Billy said, 'Thank you for coming here and letting me know all this. I'm sorry, I shoulda kept my mouth shut about it but I was drunk. I don't want you to get involved. I'd rather get this all taken care of without Chance having to think about it again either.' The implication of the last statement being, 'Chance knows something, but also don't tell Chance'.

He took another swig of his drink. 'Tell the boyfriend that I'll meet him at the club next Tuesday to talk. I think we can reason this out. Put this to bed without anyone getting hurt.'

Misty sipped her drink because that is what people do, they mimic each other to bond, and nodded at Billy's statement. She figured he was just saying something in case she was wearing a microphone.

'Do you think that is the best idea? That this guy is going to be happy with your word?' she asked, studying his face for a reaction and took another nervous sip of the drink. She needed to push it further but was worried about what he would do.

Billy finished his drink, the ice clattering around the empty glass. He thought, there is the moccasin, coming close to the surface.

'Are you mic'ed up?' he asked.

'Nope,' responded Misty. Worrying about being drugged, discussing bodily harm coming to someone with a guy who shot a girl a few weeks ago, she was getting fired up, adrenaline hitting her system. She felt like she could kick his ass if she wanted to. Not that she would try. And not that she would win.

She went on. 'I'm thinking you gave me that bullshit answer because you think I'm wired. But I'm not and no, you're not going to search me.'

'Jesus. Where do you fit into this? What's your interest?' Billy asked. He stood, eyebrows raised and shook the ice in his glass in a question to see if she wanted a refill. She shook her head and he walked to the bar.

'Well,' Misty replied, standing up, the adrenaline taking over, 'I didn't *ask* to be a part of this but you guys seem to have gotten me involved. First you tell me all about it when you were drunk, and then this guy James comes in and asks me about you and then Chance asks me about James. So I came here to deliver a message, not on a cell phone, and you give me that fluffy bullshit that everyone is going to suck each other off at the end of this. I want to know what's going to happen because he's going to give the cops my name as his contact. I'll take that drink now.' She looked up at him and added, 'What?!', her face slightly flushed.

Billy stopped in front of the bar and was smiling at her. 'You're always so controlled. Just interesting to see an actual outburst. Good to know you're human.' The last word came out 'euman', his Midwest accent coming out and sounding east coast. Misty wouldn't have known that, never being out of California.

He turned his back to her to make their drinks and went on. 'First thing I think is that we can relax a little. If the cops knew anything, Chance and I would have met a lot of them by now. Did Chance say anything about talking to the cops?' He was fishing a little to see if she'd spoken to him about their deal.

Misty, taking a step closer to the bar, watched hard to make sure Billy wasn't adding anything to her drink.

'Chance didn't say shit to me about anything,' Misty said truthfully. She didn't think Chance had been questioned but didn't know for sure. She'd have to get better at finding out information.

'Ok,' Billy said, handing Misty her second drink. 'That's good. If you didn't see cops asking questions or hanging around the place, then they don't know anything. Cops aren't subtle and don't really go undercover unless they're trying to break up a narcotics ring or some shit. But this clown James shows up. Kind of a gym rat, looks a little like Jason Bourne?'

Misty took a sip of her drink, using it to suppress a smile at the reference, not noticing that he had poured her twice as much vodka in this drink as the first one. She had been watching for Rohypnol. She sat back down on the couch and hummed an 'Umm hmm' on the glass rim and Billy went on.

'He shows up so they think I'm involved. The cops probably don't believe them since I don't have a record as an adult and they didn't ask me questions. So he stops by and talks to you.' Billy was walking around the living room, using his hands to talk as he moved, waving his drink around in between sips. 'You look young and innocent so better to talk to you than Mikey,' he said, referring to the other bartender on Tuesdays.

'Now, did he go right up to you or did he walk in and stand there for a minute?' Billy asked. Misty wasn't sure because she had her back turned but it seemed that he walked up to her first.

Misty replied, 'I think he came straight to me. I was facing the register when he came in so I'm not positive but I didn't see him go near Mikey.'

Billy pointed a finger from his drink hand at her and said, 'He knew to come to you. Did you tell anyone that I talked to you?'

'No,' Misty replied flatly. She looked at him with an expression that read, 'Do you think I'm stupid?'

'Just checking. So it was either Lauren or one of her friends.' He let that sink in for a second. 'Who's the friend that is always with Lauren at the bar?'

Misty had taken another sip of her drink and realized that it was almost finished. She put it on an end table and said, 'The wannabe. Holly? No, Molly.'

'Yes! That's it!' Billy jumped in. 'Maybe I should ask her some questions.' Billy smiles like the Grinch and Misty can see what he is thinking. 'I drove by Lauren's apartment and James' house but haven't been able to find them. They went into hiding or some shit.'

She was starting to feel a buzz and her defenses were falling away. First the hot guy, then the somewhat threatening but exciting meeting with Chance and now sitting here figuring out what's going on. It was like being in a movie. It was thrilling. Like the first time she kissed a girl. Or that time she beat her super smart 11th grade teacher at chess. These were the moments in her life that excited her, that she would always remember. Surprising, even to herself, she realized that she was starting to get aroused.

So Billy found out where James lived. He must have followed him. Being in this movie was exciting.

The actor noticed that Misty had perked up and wanted to keep her excitement level up when he replied, 'Can you find out where her friend is? I might be able to follow her to this James guy.'

'I can do that,' Misty said, feeling the urge to leave. Time's up. When Billy went to make himself a third drink, Misty excused herself and found a bathroom.

She wasn't afraid of him because he tried to kidnap Lauren or that he shot her. She knew some tough guys in Fresno growing up that weren't really bad people, just victims of their environment, like Billy. But she thought that he wasn't her type. He wasn't the reason for her wetness.

When she dated guys in high school, they were Emo or metal heads, shy and very sweet. She thought those choices were in direct contrast of Randy. But, in the end, the relationships with the nice boys didn't last. When she wound up making out with and then dating Kristi Dellenford, there was a thrill of doing something different.

She wasn't sure but thought maybe she liked the gym body on James because he could protect her? Or maybe, with all that strength, he might be rough with her...

Before leaving the bathroom, she opened her alarm app, set a timer for 6 minutes in the future and set the ringer to vibrate. She flushed the standing water and went back to the sofa.

Billy had put on some low music and possibly dimmed the lights a little. He was starting to talk about what to do next when Misty's timer went off. She pulled her phone out of her small bag, hit the cancel timer button, held the phone up to her ear and in a friendly voice said, 'Hey what's up?' to no one.

Billy stopped talking and waited. Misty said, 'Really?' Then 'Shit, I'm on my way.' She stood up and headed for the door. 'It looks like I took the keys for register two when I left. I have to go back.' She rifled around in her bag for effect.

Billy was a little crestfallen as he walked her out. He said, 'You can come back,' and realized that it sounded a little desperate, even to his ears. She didn't address that, instead saying, 'I'll see if I can find out more about the friend, Molly.'

She drove straight to her small, first floor one-bedroom apartment, which was on a nice street near the border of a sketchy neighborhood. She parked in her assigned spot, unlocked and relocked her front door and strode straight into her bedroom, dropping her keys and bag on the floor on the way.

When she was in bed and naked, she tried to focus on some of the things that had happened during the day that have gotten her excited. The meeting with Chance was pretty hot, but scary. The conversation with Billy about being forceful to Molly was good too, even though she didn't like the idea of *really* hurting anyone. But, in the end, the thing that did it for her was the thought of James tearing her underwear off and bending her over the hood of the Aston.

-

James had filled Lauren in on the conversation with Misty at the Katana when he got home last night. She was happy that he found out stuff but was worried about how involved it was becoming, even though he said that there was a total lack of drama.

15.

James wakes up early, ready for his routine and realizes that he's not at the Hermosa house and he doesn't have his small gym. He has a membership to a nice club and a boxing gym, and uses both regularly, but today he was looking forward to getting in forty-five minutes in the garage. Damn.

Since he can remember, his workouts were always a combination of things. He would do cardio every day and would add arms and chest one day, quads and glutes the next, abs and calves, shoulders, etc. He always worked multiple groups, making sure not to overwork a section or underwork an area.

He used to go to his friend's dojo and practice a weird combination of martial arts and common-sense fighting but stopped going last year, as he was not really being a fan of sparring. He went for 10 years and liked learning the moves but was always worried about hurting forty-year-old Dave from accounting who went twice a month to get away from the wife and kids. It never occurred to James to be afraid of getting hurt.

James was fast. He moved fast and had fast hands. He assumed it was just due to youth and his high school football days but it went well beyond that. He had never been tackled from behind when he played. He adjusted to incoming would-be tacklers with almost clairvoyant reflexes. He assumed that he was a normal tailback, that he was just as fast as kids from the other teams, but that wasn't exactly correct.

During his senior year, he scored more touchdowns during regular season games than some other *teams* had, taking his team to the state championship. After their best wide receiver was hurt on the third offensive play, they lost to a good defensive team from somewhere in Northern California who were able to key in on him for most of the game.

His favorite play of the game was captured on camera, where he took a screen pass to the weak side and hurdled the defender like he was sliding across the hood of a car. Like Starsky and Hutch, his mom would have said. He was taken down in the secondary by the safety and a corner back after picking up twenty-nine yards and setting them up for a rushing touchdown. He scored 3 TDs through double coverage.

James did what he could in the living room at 6:30am with no weights. Push-ups, burpees, shadow boxing, crunches and some Pilates. He worked for forty minutes doing power sets, going from one right into another without breaks. To him, cardio was just as important as weights. What good was looking in shape if you got winded after 10 minutes on a bike?

-

Lauren wakes up feeling physically better each day. Her mom sees the improvements and, while standing in the palatial kitchen drinking coffee, she tells her that she'll head back up the coast in a few days. Lauren starts to think about going home herself, back to her apartment in Sherman Oaks. She feels guilty for thinking it, thinking that James has been amazing and sweet and has paid for *everything* but is slightly worried about losing her independence.

As if reading her mind, Tori, looking over the rim of her cup, says, 'You're going to go back to your apartment when this is all over? That might cause a problem with you two.'

Lauren looks toward the living room where the stairs are, knowing that James is probably in the shower. In a low tone, she says, 'I'm thinking about that. I feel like I spent my whole life building up to be the person I was and I've been on vacation from that for the past 5 weeks. It's been great but vacations have to end sometime.'

Eyebrows raised, Tori warns, 'Think about how you are going to say that so you don't hurt him. He's fully invested. You look like you might be too but you have always been fiercely independent, like your dad.'

'Thanks mom,' Lauren says and feels her emotions well up a little. She gives Tori a half smile that is a little wrinkled at the thought of her dad and leans in for a hug.

James walks into the kitchen while they are hugging and goes right in without hesitation, hugging Lauren to her mother. He holds it for a two-count and heads to the coffee machine. Lauren and Tori exchange a smile and a quick glance and Tori announces her plan to pack and shower and makes her way out of the kitchen.

Lauren decides not to bring it up yet, since the danger is far from over. Maybe she'll change her mind. She was worried that the banter will stop, that the fun back-and-forth rhythm they established, would be strangled by the awkwardness. She wasn't aware how much she wanted to be with someone smart, someone quick-witted, before now.

16.

During a Friday meeting with his business manager/lawyer/uncle Max, James gets a text from Misty on the burner, which he left in the car. When he gets back, the phone is hot from the sun but he carefully unlocks it.

- Meet tonight at the Katana at 8 -M

He hadn't heard from Mila the detective or Willie Bard the investigator yet and thinks, it will be a crowded bar. What could happen?

He checks in with the security lead Kenny and asks if he or anyone else on the team has seen anything suspicious or noticed anyone following Lauren. Kenny replies, 'Negative. All quiet.' James doesn't tell Kenny his plan but makes sure the detail stays on Lauren.

He tells Lauren when he gets back that he has a meet with Misty at the bar at 8. Lauren wants to go along but James makes a funny face at her and looks at her still-healing belly. He values her people insight but there is no way that he would put her in danger. He doesn't say it though.

'What about you?' she asked. She had been thinking about her conversation with her mom in the kitchen, about her independence, about how the 'return to real life' conversation is going to go. A small part of her subconscious pulled back from James, afraid to get hurt if their talk went bad. She doesn't want him to get killed, of course, but is willing to let him manage himself a little also.

Lauren: 'I thought you weren't going to investigate.'

James: 'I wasn't but no one else seems to be doing anything. I don't want to just sit around and wait for you to get shot again.'

He's waiting for Lauren to push back or to show concern but neither of those things happen. She doesn't move in closer, doesn't ask him to stay home, doesn't try to change his mind, just tells him to be careful.

He senses the difference in Lauren. Under-protectiveness? Is that a word? For the first time in their relationship, he tells her a lie and says that Kenny will have someone go with him. He's not thinking about the danger when he kisses her and heads out, only about the almost imperceptible shift that seems to have happened.

After the betrayal he felt from Becca, his high school girlfriend that cheated on him, James has been somewhat protective of himself. He dated and let a few women get close but was always looking out for red flags, breaking it off whenever he thought he saw one. He didn't see any from Becca and assumed that, since he was in love, that he wasn't looking carefully enough. He wouldn't make that mistake again.

He subconsciously simmered on it for the whole ride to the Katana.

-

Lauren wishes her mom had stayed a little longer to keep her company tonight and calls Molly, who says, 'I'll come for a little bit. Have some plans at ten though.' Lauren thanks her and wonders what plans she has for 10pm. She does not make plans for 10pm but it seems normal for Molly to.

Lauren dutifully informs Kenny to expect her, and he tells the team.

-

James shows up at the Katana about ten minutes early and parks the Rivian in a spot along the side of the place. He heads over to Misty's side of the bar and sits.

'Hey,' she smiles at him.

'Hey,' he replies.

She's wearing a soft-looking, black, low-cut shirt and stretch jeans with a pair of black Nikes. Her hair is in loose curls and she's wearing glasses, which James comments on.

'I like your glasses,' he says, as a conversation opener, thinking that, 'Your ass makes those jeans look awesome' is probably not appropriate for this girl or given his current relationship status. But both are true. He does like the glasses and her ass is making the jeans look great.

Also, her smile reaches her eyes today and makes her look less like she's hiding a knife somewhere.

'Thanks,' she said shyly, not pretending to be shy but feeling a little flushed at the compliment. No one would ever accuse Misty of being shy or girlie, but she felt like a high school girl meeting the star quarterback, even though she never felt like that in high school about football players.

He's wearing jeans and a black button-up shirt that shows off his strong arms. She asks what he wants to drink and looks at his upper body quickly. He notices.

'An 805, please.'

She goes to get a bottle of Firestone 805, moving a little more slowly than the last time he was here. She gets a bottle from the under-counter fridge, bending at the waist, knees locked, giving James a view of her from behind. He watches her for a second and then looks around the bar, thinking that he shouldn't be looking for that long. She peeked at him in the mirror behind the bar right before she bent and saw him looking, smiling to herself.

She picks up a frosted pint glass on the way back to James with his beer, opening it with the flat opener from her back pocket and flipping the cap into an unseen garbage can. She placed them in front of James and asked, 'How's your day going?'

'Work, lawyer stuff, the usual,' James replied, trying to make sure the attention is not focused on what he does for work. Since he would receive varying requests from strangers like 'Can I get cheap rent?' or 'Do you have anything I can rent near the beach?', it was something he learned to keep private. While he liked helping people, he found that acquaintances imposed more than anyone else. 'How has your week been?'

Misty put a hand on the bar and leaned forward on her toes, turning her head to the side, getting close to James' face and showing him a little cleavage, in a conspiratorial tone said, 'I found out some more information.'

James leaned slightly forward to meet her and Misty leaned a little more forward to match. He smelled her perfume and it triggered memory remnants, still pictures of another very attractive girl, her skin against his, her head back. He didn't recall exactly who that was at the moment but he pushed the memory aside as quickly as he could.

She thought for a minute about how to approach the situation. Hmm.

'Since he couldn't find you, he is going to try and find Lauren's friend, Holly,' Misty said quietly, intentionally using the wrong name for Molly. Her hope was to sound like an outsider, digging up information to help James.

'I didn't think of that. Shit,' James said, feeling stupid for not protecting Molly.

'I don't know if he can find her. I don't think he is that smart,' Misty adds.

James pulls his personal phone and starts texting Kenneth. 'She's always out in Hollywood so I'm pretty sure that anyone can find her.'

As Misty heads down the bar to help a 40-ish looking couple, she thinks about how James immediately pulled his phone and started working out how to protect that girl, Molly. The thought of him going out of his way to help someone else strikes her as naïve, innocent. People don't do that anymore, she thinks, but also thinks that she could use his naivete to move him away from Lauren.

James texts Kenneth and asks for his detail to pick up Molly. Kenneth texts back and says that he is already watching Molly and James realizes that they are probably dating, or something like that.

Sipping his beer, James watches Misty as she reaches up on her tiptoes to grab a bottle that is high up on a back bar shelf. She pours whiskey into a small glass for the guy and shakes out an espresso martini for the lady, smiling that smile that doesn't reach her eyes as she takes their credit card and swipes it, leaving the tab open. As the couple turn back toward each other, she turns and heads back down the bar toward James, thinking about what she can say to turn his attention to her. He takes care of that before she reaches him.

'Thank you for finding this out for me. It is very nice of you. Please make sure you are not putting yourself in any danger, okay?'

Misty watched James take out his phone and send something as soon as she mentioned that Molly might be in danger. She wonders about that. Maybe the protectiveness is because he is sleeping with Molly also?... Possible, but not probable since he was being protective of her too. But the possibility makes her fantasy a little hotter.

She thinks she knows what to do, how to appeal to him. 'I'm only doing the right thing. Besides, I like you,' she says, leaving the sentence open-ended. She says it in a way that could mean that she likes him as a friend or she likes him as more than that. She'll let him decide what to do with it.

Since James finds Misty attractive, he takes it as more-than-friends. He's pretty sure that most of the world's population would find Misty attractive. As he is about to state his relationship status with Lauren, he stops. The doubt creeps in after his and Lauren's most recent conversation and, 'I like you, too,' comes out of his mouth before he can stop it.

There is a very long two second pause where they lock eyes. They both smile a little and Misty blushes, turning her head shyly down and to the left. She feels a thrum in her lower abdomen and, her smile widening says, 'Dude, you made me blush!', which is true. She walks down the bar to get James another 805.

James, momentarily happy with himself for being able to attract someone like Misty, feels guilt and regret watching her walk back to him. She seemed happy, which he hadn't seen before. She always wore a look of boredom or indifference, it seemed. Showing perfect upper teeth, her big smile makes her go from pretty to absolutely stunning. Her face seems to glow with it, making her look simultaneously younger and more like a woman.

James' guilt is temporarily forgotten because of that smile.

When she gets back in front of him with the beer and a new cold glass, she flips the cap off into the unseen garbage can again and pours it. James, still a little pink in the cheeks, attempts to get himself out of the cloud that her smile put him in. 'Thanks for the beer. How did you find this out?'

Misty, who practically floated over with the beer, was brought down a little by the turn of focus away from the her-and-James conversation and back to Billy. She planned this answer in advance, knowing that she would not be able to say that she found out from his couch while drinking his vodka.

'I have a friend that works at that Bigfoot-themed bar called Yeti, on Melrose. She said Billy went in there asking about Molly last week. She thought maybe Billy liked her and was looking for a date.'

James asked, 'Is that the place that plays old reel-to-reel home movies on the pull-down screen?' Molly was nodding so he went on. 'So what do you think he'll do if he finds her?'

'I don't know,' Misty replies, pretending to be deep in thought but her brain is thinking like the game Battleship, firing off test shots to see where his pieces are on the board. 'I think we need to call the police.' She's hoping that her drastic change from the no-bullshit girl to this concerned, flirty girl four days later isn't too drastic and gets noticed.

'Ah, I did that. I don't think they found out anything. No witnesses, no cameras in the parking lot where she was shot. I hired an investigator too but they only dig up background.'

Thanks for the information, Misty thinks. She hadn't told Billy that James was going to be here, which is good. She's thinking about how to get Billy out of the picture without taking down Chance. If there is a fight, James wouldn't kill Bill. He's too nice. Billy would most certainly shoot James though.

But she really didn't want James to get shot...

They talked for another hour while James had two more beers. They did a shot together (Misty doing a real shot this time) and James decided to try out the Autopilot in the Rivian. He thought about an Uber but figured he was okay.

He said goodbye to Misty for a little too long and headed out to his car. The parking lot was semi-enclosed, with an ivy-covered fence on one side and a concrete block wall separating the lot from an apartment complex on the other. The back of the lot was open to a small side street.

-

Molly comes in with Kenneth, both looking a little flirty.

Kenny closes the door behind her. Molly is wearing a see-through-ish white dress, back-and-white Cheshire Cat shoes and a *very* self-satisfied smile.

‘So,’ she starts with, ‘You didn’t *really* tell me about the sex...’

Lauren has never been the person that talks about sex or bathroom things or bodily functions of any sort. She did talk about sex when she was with Molly to some extent but never the way Molly would or wanted to.

‘Oh it’s really good. He’s, a, giver,’ she settles on, thinking that explanation would work.

Molly, palms raised, shoulders shrugged, said, ‘He gives what, good advice? Hugs? I need more than that.’

Lauren is a little embarrassed. She says, ‘He likes to make sure I’m satisfied. A. LOT. OF. TIMES.’

‘*Really.* Damn that’s hot. I’ve actually found the opposite recently, a guy who just sort of *takes*, which is fucking hot too.’

Lauren looks at Molly intently for a second, looks at the door that she came in through and back at Molly, who smiles.

Instead of asking questions, she goes back to herself. ‘It’s really good but I think he wants to keep the lights on more...’

Molly’s head turns to the side like when a puppy hears a dog bark out of a cell phone. ‘Why would you not have the lights on for him? You know guys are visual and you, you look like that,’ gesturing to all of Lauren.

‘Well I have this pooch thing here,’ she says, looking down at her lower belly.

‘Bitch no. I have seen you naked like a thousand times. You’ve got a booty, boobs and the flat stomach of a gymnast, and you *barely* work out. I’m not a ‘bo but I thought about what to do with you once or twice.’

Lauren looked at Molly for a beat, then Molly continued. ‘And,’ she said, ‘if he’s doing all that for you, you should have the lights on AND be in the mirror. Hide a camera for that guy!’

Lauren was slightly embarrassed but laughed. Molly was relentless.

‘Everybody likes hot, half Hawaiian girls...’

'So what is Kenny like?' Lauren asked, smiling conspiratorially and quickly changing the subject from her heritage to Molly.

'Uh, have you seen that?' Molly throws a thumb at the door she came in. 'He's built like a pro wide receiver. And he knows how to handle himself so he's got a confidence that I have never seen before.'

Molly adds, 'But that's not gonna work. Nice distraction though. Tell me, how many times has he made you come in one night?'

Lauren blushed. Molly is the only person who could ask her questions like this and she would answer. She looked at her feet and said, 'I lost track last time after eight.'

'*EIGHT*?!?' Molly said. 'Wait, no. You said you lost track *after* eight. Girl, after fucking eight I would have erected a shrine of him in my bedroom!'

Lauren laughed, which hurt and she held her staples when she laughed.

Molly, sincere, asked 'Can I borrow him for a little bit before the 'Little Sister' contract kicks in?'

'No!' replies Lauren, pretending to be aghast.

'Okaaayy', Molly draws out, then, 'so why did you really invite me? Are you worried about being alone?'

Lauren: 'Just the opposite.'

Molly: 'WHAT?! You don't want to be with *that* guy? Talk, woman.'

Lauren: 'It's not that. He's wonderful.' She goes out of her way to not use the word 'but'. 'I'm just so used to being independent. And this happened so fast it's like I'm married already. I wasn't expecting that.'

Molly: 'Just so I have this straight. You are going to end it with the guy who rescued you from a kidnapping by going full Batman into the bad guys, who is built better than marble statues of Greek gods, who has tons of money and can make your eyes roll back into your head several times a night? What am I missing here? What aren't you telling me about him?'

Lauren: 'No, there doesn't seem to be any skeletons in his closet. Only thing is his ex made him cautious.'

Molly gives Lauren a flat look that says 'Really?'

Lauren continues: 'It's not him, it's me. This was too much too fast. I just want to slow it down a little, not end it.'

Molly: 'That's not going to work. You are either going to stay with him and have a great life or break up with him so I can wear his ass like a hat.'

Lauren, confused: 'What does that even mean?'

Molly, wearing a sly smile: '*You know what it means.* Seriously though, you're taking a chance that he will end it. He's gone over-and-above what people would do for their family, no less a girl. Even if you are hot. And half Japanese? Pushing back might feel like pushing him away, especially if he is cautious.'

Lauren: 'You're right but I don't see a way around it. I'm happy but also smothering a little like I'm claustrophobic.'

Molly: 'My opinion, you are making a terrible mistake and I do not condone it. BUT I'm here for you. AND I am going to try and make sure you guys find your way back to each other. If you guys do break up forever, I will not be held accountable for my actions, so don't be surprised if you find a picture of me on all fours on his back naked. Just assume there was a horrible accident.'

Lauren, chuckling: 'What? Why would you, you know what, never mind. I don't want to know.'

-

James reconsidered his plan to drive when Billy stepped out from between the Rivian and the car next to him and swung a left at James. James, a little impaired but still impossibly fast, dodged the swing and moved a little away to try and gets some perspective on what was happening.

Billy threw a right that connected with James' temple and James stumbled, off balance for a second. This seemed like the opening Billy needed and he stepped toward James, who unexpectedly moved back towards Billy, bringing his fists up next to his head in a classic fighting stance.

James thought he saw something heavy moving in Billy's hoodie pocket and thought it might be a gun. I'd better make him keep his hands up, James thought. If James went down, he figured Billy would shoot him. The adrenaline dump he got from that thought pushed the alcohol and temple punch out of James' head and he was fully alert.

Billy was around 5'8" and James a solid 5'10". They were evenly matched in height and reach but James had at least 30 pounds on the wiry Billy.

Billy threw a left-right combination that James blocked, the bony, rock-climber knuckles of Billy's hands hurting James' forearms. James countered with a straight right hand that grazed Billy's chin. Billy was aware that James almost got him on the chin but figured James got lucky.

Both wary, they danced for three seconds, watching each other's movements. Billy thought he could get inside on James, so he tucked his arms in and tried to catch James with an upper cut.

When James saw Billy's elbows tuck in, he understood where he was going. He side-stepped to his left quickly and threw his left elbow at where he thought Billy's head would be. The elbow pushed Billy's fist into his own head and Billy stepped to his own left to try and avoid most of the impact. It didn't completely work.

Billy's next thought was, how fast was that? He didn't think he saw James move. Couldn't be. Billy shook his head slightly to shake off a little of the ringing that he felt when James moved on him.

James, guard up in his fighting stance, stepped in and grabbed Billy's left wrist with his right hand. James' left grabbed a chunk of shirt and hoodie with his left at Billy's collar. He took a half step backward, planted his right foot onto Billy's hip and rolled down and backward. Since he outweighed Billy, he didn't need Billy's momentum to pull off the move he had planned.

Since he thought he was going to fall onto James, Billy tried to put his hands out towards the ground to stop his fall. But that didn't happen. The foot on the hip helped James launch Billy over into a perfect

Tomoe Nage Judo throw, Billy flying upside down for what seemed like an eternity to him.

Billy landed on the back of his neck, pulling his head up into a tuck at the very last second, with his back hitting flat on the parking lot concrete next. He jumped up before his feet had really hit and scrambled over the 6' cinder block wall opposite of the space he came out of, running down an alley next to an apartment complex.

James was up quickly but didn't expect Billy to run in the opposite direction that fast. He did not give chase since Billy may have had time to pull the gun after he scaled the wall.

He listened, thinking that he maybe should run somewhere public, but heard Billy's footfalls fading on the other side of the wall.

James went back into the Katana to be around people in case Billy came back to shoot him and to maybe get some ice for his head.

While he was walking, he thought, did she know? Did Misty know Billy was going to be there?

James walked back in and walked toward the bar. He was thinking about what he was going to say when Misty looked over in the way that all bar staff look at people who walk in, are they going to be trouble, are they already drunk, do I know them.

Misty's mouth dropped open when she saw James. He looked disheveled with his shirt out of place, his perfect hair messed up and a lump/bruise starting to form on his head. She not-quite-ran to him, picked up his right hand in her left and put her right hand on his face, looking at his temple. She guided him into a bar stool and asked if he was alright.

James saw the look of concern and knew she didn't set up the ambush. Either that or she was the best actress in a town full of good actresses. But Misty didn't seem like an actress. She seemed like the person who told you too much, who didn't know how to hold back.

She went and got some ice from behind the bar for his head, wrapping it in a new bar towel so that is didn't smell like old booze, and walked back around to him. She took a better look at his head and placed the ice pack there gently. He took it and she put her hand on his chest.

'Billy?' She asked, eyebrows knitted together, forming three vertical lines in her forehead. 'I'm sorry,' she added when he nodded and then winced from moving his head.

She went back behind the bar, looked for aspirin, didn't find any and poured him a shot. She took care of him for the next twenty minutes, changing his ice, his towel, getting him a beer, touching him frequently.

While she was doing this, Misty thought a few things to herself. Her first thought was genuine concern for James. She realized that she actually felt something for him in her heart.

The second thought was, I'm going to have to erase the video of this.

James recounted the fight to her, as people do after an adrenaline-fueled event, but without bragging. He lived in a town full of braggers and self-promoters but did none of that himself. He usually stayed quiet while others did. Either that or he told a similar, funny story. When that failed, he changed the subject to something else like sports.

When he told Misty about the Tomoe Nage, Misty stopped bustling around him, took a step back and asked, 'Uh, whatsthatnow?'

When he repeated it, it sounded a little crazy to his ears. During a fight with a (likely armed) man, he pulled off a risky, complicated Judo throw that is rarely seen in fighting. He blushed a little at the way she was looking at him.

He hung his head. 'That might have been stupid. I didn't really think about it, I just thought that would shake things up. I didn't want him to feel comfortable in his style of fighting but didn't really want to hurt hm.'

'Just so I have this right, you *threw* a grown-ass man,' Misty says point blank. 'Shake things up' is a major understatement. He's going to shoot first next time.'

James says, 'It's not the first stupid thing I've done.'

'Let's make sure it is not your last,' Misty said. She's curious about his stories though. She smiles at him, gives the come-on gesture with her fingers and says, 'Tell me. I love to hear the stupid shit other people do.'

While she dabs at his head with the towel, he tells her how he came across a burning house. He got out of his car, and while running full speed, he threw a rock through a picture window and then jumped through it. He called out for anyone inside, running through the burning house with his shirt covering his face but found no people. He found a cat hiding in a corner, grabbed it and ran out through the front door, which was standing open four feet from the window he jumped through.

When he was fifteen, he went surfing in some big swells with a friend near Santa Monica in the late afternoon. While just past the breakers, he saw a girl out swimming inside the crash zone that was struggling to keep her head above water. He paddled over to help and got her onto his board. While towing her in, the current pulled them toward the pier and he got smashed between the pylons, the barnacles tearing him up. If he would have angled them toward the beach, they would have missed the pier altogether.

Misty listened to this, occasionally pausing him to help other patrons. She thought, he thinks he looks stupid in these stories but he's a fucking superhero.

-

Kenny received James' text about Molly but obviously had a plan together already on how to protect her already. Whoever these guys are, they are very amateur, but even amateurs can pull a trigger, so he would keep Molly close. And maybe for personal reasons also.

No one was going through Kenny to get to Molly.

-

When James gets home, Lauren takes one look at his face and became upset. She went to med school and has seen the human body in some ugly states, a lot worse than this, but got an uncomfortable feeling about seeing James with bruises.

She knows he's human but feels that he really hasn't really been human since she has met him. He was super-human, impervious to injury. Hell, he drove into a van to save her and hadn't been touched. He was also good-looking, funny (jocular, in fact!) and dressed well. She went to get ice for him, the concern like butterflies in her stomach.

She asked what happened and James recounted the story for her. While he talked, she pictured the parking lot, the fence, the car, someone jumping out. While he talked, her interest changed from, 'Was my person about to get hurt' to 'What made him not only think he could execute that move but how did he actually throw a grown man ass-over-tea-kettle through a parking lot'. She asked questions.

'So how fast was the throw?' she asked. 'Did he have time to react?'

Somewhere in her subconscious, the scientist in her went nuts. She had always wanted to ask questions to the people she saw in videos that could jump from rooftops and land on walls or slide down poles. How does that work to those who have the physical prowess to pull those moves off?

James explained that they seemed to be testing each other out a little when, in his subconscious, he thought Billy was moving somewhat slow. So he described the throw, which he thought was also a little slow. He left out the fact that Misty had given him ice for his head, the way she touched his chest. He didn't want to hide anything but felt there was really nothing to hide. He thought that, but he also thought he was hiding it.

-

Saturday morning, over a simple at-home breakfast of toast and juice, Lauren decided to go and stay with her mom for a week. She feels conflicted now, trying to keep a small space around herself but caring for James a lot at the same time. As she packed, the conversation became a little awkward but they both thought it might be for the best, for entirely different reasons.

'Just temporarily, right?' James asked, eyebrows raised.

'Of course,' Lauren replied, 'I think something is going to happen here soon and I don't really want to get shot again.'

'Is it okay if I send a detail with you?'

Lauren replied with, 'You'd better' and smiled to lighten the mood.

17.

Misty calls Chance and tells him that Billy fucked up the fight. Chance flips out, as he does. With the phone pressed to her ear, she listens to him breaking things, cursing. After a few seconds, she pushes the 'End' button on her phone and goes back to what she was doing.

Currently she is hanging out with Elizabeth Crawley, a divorced, forty-something, washed-up Hollywood attorney who has a drinking problem and a somewhat-to-severe crush on Misty. From what people say, she was a big deal in the movie industry until her fall from grace four years ago.

Liz told Misty that she had been out for after-work drinks with a few of Hollywood's elite to celebrate the closing of a very large studio deal. She left early, after only a few drinks, but was tired from all the long hours it took to get the deal made. She nodded off slightly on Hollywood Boulevard and drove into a police car that was double parked. Both officers claimed injuries and both went on permanent disability but she spoke to witnesses that claim that they were on the sidewalk talking to a homeless man.

According to her story, the judge did not care much for the witnesses because 'A' they were homeless people and '2' she was legally drunk at the time. She was unceremoniously fired from her firm for having a conviction and served her sentence by reporting to prison every weekend for two years. Her husband left her during that time, looking to find someone with less problems (and more money).

To her credit, she hid half of her money from him before the accident since he was such a flake. Pretty but flaky.

Misty thinks that parts of that story are true because she gets animated at the witness part but reads the rest like a script she wrote. She contradicts herself on occasion as well, citing at times that they went out at noon and she hit the police car at night.

Misty didn't care about that. Liz was her only real friend and was very nice to her. Humans make mistakes. She shouldn't still be punishing herself. Also, she knows Liz has a crush on her and, while Liz is a little out of her age range, it is nice to have someone who is slightly enamored by you.

Even though they don't have a lot in common, they have stayed up late on a number of occasions at Liz's two-bedroom Hollywood Hills stilt house, drinking (mostly Liz) into the early hours and talking.

Liz was the only person outside of Fresno that Misty had told about her assault.

-

Chance decides that he might be able to get three or four people to beat this guy up but doesn't tell Misty or Billy about it.

Through another bouncer, Chance gets the name and number of a borderline psycho he knows about that sometimes works the door and gentlemen's clubs. David Prince is neither a gentleman or a prince. He's a 6'2" tall gym rat who thinks that the world is out to get him and that he needs to be prepared. He wants to have an arsenal of weapons and black belt skills but has neither. His condescending attitude towards people and over-confidence in general does not match his low intelligence or his lack of fighting ability.

He was private security for some of the Hollywood elite for a while but would be too aggressive with fans or paparazzi, usually hurting them in front of the celebrity. Celebrities do not like that and he was unanimously uninvited to industry work after breaking a photographer's wrist.

The $5,000 Chance is offering up is good and he knows who to call for backup. Dave calls two other friends he knows who will rough a person up for money and one brings his younger brother, Scooter. Since no one knows where to find James, they decide to catch him outside his gym one morning.

Dave and his three friends park themselves in the parking lot outside of the Equinox gym in Santa Monica and wait for James. They each have duffel bags or backpacks, like they finished working out and are just chatting. Dave matches the security camera picture he has from the Blue Katana and spotted James working out. They will surround James and ask him about Lauren in an attempt to confuse him about her.

From his vantage point on the second floor, James sees the men in the parking lot easily through the massive, 3-story front windows. They look around too much and don't have the relaxed posture of guys who are shooting the breeze. They look tense.

Also, at this time in the morning on a Monday, people have places to go. They don't sit in a parking lot outside the gym not talking very much.

Since Lauren wasn't with him, he gave the detail that stayed in LA the daytime hours off, not thinking for a minute that somebody would come for him at 7am.

He leaves his gear in a locker and heads to his car. When he steps through the doors, all four of the men move to form a circle around him, which he expected. The leader, a large white guy with crazy eyes, says to him, 'We want to talk to you about Lauren...'

James takes two very fast, short steps to the leader (he thinks of him as the leader since he spoke first) bringing up his right hand. He turns his hips and hit the leader in the jaw with an open palm strike like an uppercut, delivering forearm-bone-to-jaw force that he learned in class. The leader's head turned up and to the left rapidly from the impact, which separated his jaw and knocked him unconscious.

Before the leader's unconscious bulk hit the ground, James, still moving, shifts to his left and puts his left hand in front of the next attacker's face. The second guy, in sweats and a gray Adidas shirt doesn't see the big wind up of the right. James drops down into a squat and rises up using his legs and swings up with his right fist, which strikes Sweatpants in the solar plexus. James forces the fist up and under the ribs as hard as he can, using his body weight to lift the man off the ground a little.

The strike knocks the wind out of Sweatpants and he goes down, holding his abdomen and sucking in air.

Scooter, nicknamed as such by his bullying older brother for riding the same scooter even when he became too big for it, thought they were there to intimidate someone, maybe rough him up a little, maybe not. He was the largest of the men. When he saw the speed and force that their target moved, he took off running. He didn't want any part of whatever this shit was.

His older brother Dusty, also a nickname, was mean. He was a cat kicker, a bully. He was going to teach this guy a lesson. His self-preservation had not kicked in yet like his little brother's did, even though he just dropped the two other strong guys he was with.

As James moved to his left, the attackers were less of a circle and more of a line now, especially with Scooter breaking the circle.

But Dusty knew he was faster than these other muscle-heads. Dusty stepped toward James as James was turning toward him and threw a fast right hand. James stepped quickly toward Dusty, left foot forward, and put up a left arm to block.

Since he'd studied how people fight, how they attack, James knew that 89% of people were right-handed, despite their fight training. So, if your opponent was right-handed, their stronger hand was always the right. While he himself was ambidextrous, he knew to plan for attackers to favor their right side.

So when Dusty threw a left, James didn't work hard to block it. He threw up a right arm, stepped and shot a left fist at Dusty's rib cage, just under his pectoral, breaking a rib.

Dusty didn't feel the pain before he countered, trying to land an overhand right, which James easily side-stepped by moving to his own right slightly.

When the pain hit Dusty, James threw a fast three punch combination that hit Dusty in the ribs, chin and right temple, in that order. He stepped again to his right and watched as Dusty folded up on himself, holding his midsection as he went down.

James looked around for other attackers, knowing that there were at least four but saw one take off. The entire event lasted maybe five seconds. To James, it felt like 15 minutes.

James had not said a word throughout the fight.

With no one getting up, James calmly walked to his Rivian. Without looking back, he hopped in and drove off.

-

Monterey Jones, an influencer with 1.2 million followers on Instagram alone, was out front recording herself in front of the upscale gym doing her pre-workout routine. She did this almost daily. She set up a tripod in the parking lot and filmed herself going into the gym, showing off her abs and butt as much as possible. Whenever she showcases those, she gets 3-4x as many hits as she would normally. So, sex sells. Everyone knew that. She was making six figures from YouTube and the brands she wore and was unsuccessfully trying to get Equinox to sponsor her gym fees.

Her video recorded everything that happened in front of the gym on the left side of the frame and her, closer, on the right. She saw it coming together on her screen and watched the short fight. When it was over, she picked up the tripod and recorded James walking to his car. When he closed the door of the Rivian, she pointed the camera at her face and quoted, 'Jesus Christ,' short pause, 'that's Jason Bourne.'

The video went viral in minutes. Most people thought it was staged because the action was so fast, but they couldn't explain how one person could be sped up while the other five, including Monty, weren't.

The police acquired a copy of the security camera footage from Equinox, confirming the ambush and corroborating the viral video. A few hours later, the security footage was leaked to the public by the counter clerk, Mason, who maintained a severe crush on Monty Jones and wanted to prove her video was authentic.

-

On the video, James was as cool as a cucumber, walking away from the destruction that were his would-be attackers. On the inside, James his mind was the table of a pinball machine with all of the metal balls rolling around at the same time. How had he bested three large men who were obviously there as the predators? He thinks about the moves, most of which he had practiced, but it wasn't about that. It came down to sympathy. He really didn't want to hurt Billy or Dave from Accounting from his martial arts classes or even other football players in high school but he didn't care if he hurt those guys.

James was numb while walking to the car. He knew exactly what he had done and that he hadn't seriously injured anyone. His shots had landed perfectly. But he just couldn't process how he had taken down three large guys so easily. Were they that bad or was he that good?

As he was driving away, completely unaware of Monty Jones and her recording or quotes, he called Kenny, told him what happened and asked what he should do next.

Kenny told him, 'Looks like the hard part is already done, my guy. I'll get some people around you now.'

He was in the Rivian for fifteen minutes on his way back to the Santa Monica house when his phone buzzed. Edgar texted him and wrote, 'You are on the internets' and sends a link to the video of him outside the gym.

That was fast, James thought.

-

Misty starts to think that she is in a little over her head. There are potential problems with the three guys. Chance, who is probably a rapist, Billy, who shot Lauren Parker, and James, who is strong. If any of them feel like she is setting them up, they'll hurt her. She isn't going to get hurt. Not going to let anything like that happen again.

Worried about being in the middle of this mess, she gets a ghetto gun from her brother's friend Daryl, who is so broke he can't afford a second "R" or "L" in his name like everyone else. She thinks the gun is going to blow up in her face and kill her but Daryl says that it'll work. It's been tested. She's not sure how to feel about that. Who had been shot by this piece of crap already? Does having it make her part of a different crime, other than illegally having a gun? She hopes not.

She hefts the gun and thinks she may need to practice with it. She's not sure where she could do that in LA without being seen. She forgets the practice since she thinks she's not going to use it unless she has to. And if that is the case, the guy will probably be right on top of her.

She also thinks that Hollywood people are just as ghetto as Fresno people but with nicer cars.

18.

The fog moving through the fir and redwood trees, the books, the company with her mom that never really entered the awkward child-parent stage, are all wonderful. The record player spins dramatic, unpopular classical music. The hushed sounds from the ocean a few blocks away. All add to the general coziness of her mom's place. The only exception being the Herman Miller Eames lounge chair near the picture window and bookshelves, which makes her miss her father.

When she arrived in Carmel, she thought that she was making the right decision, putting a little space in between herself and James. Being dependent on a guy like that made her nervous.

And although she is comfortably ensconced in her mother's cottage-style home in Carmel, Lauren misses James. His easy manner, his strong arms wrapped around her. She is anxious, the lounge chair continually bringing her up out of her mental fog, reminding her of the frailty of life.

He may be fast but bullets are faster. She decides she'll go back, that she can't sit here and just wait for him to get killed. Even if they don't stay together, she will care for him the way he has cared for her.

-

James calls Lauren and tells her about the 'confrontation', as James has started calling it. Lauren looks online for a few minutes and comes up with the video, amazed by what she sees. How is this her guy? How did she not know he was capable of moving like that?

While talking with Lauren, James' phone rings with another call, the number unavailable on the caller ID. He tells Lauren he will call her back in a few minutes. James clicks over to the other call and finds it is Detective Mila.

'Hi James,' she says, 'how are you?'

James didn't think it was a coincidence that she was calling but didn't know how someone recognized him and let her know so quickly. He thought it was probably facial recognition.

'I'm okay. I got ambushed outside the gym this morning though, that wasn't so great.'

Mila: 'Looks like it was okay for you but maybe not so okay for the ambushers. Where did you learn those moves?'

James is quiet for a second, a little shy, and Mila continued with, 'And can you teach me? Wow.'

One police interview tactic is making friends with the interviewee. Complimenting them. Getting them to trust you to talk to them. Mila was good at it but there were better in her department. She didn't normally have the patience for it but, in this case, was actually interested in what James had done to three attackers.

James: 'I have taken a lot of classes. Most of what I have learned is about being ready and how to get myself out of situations just like that one.'

Mila: 'It didn't seem like anyone was seriously hurt.' She knew for a fact that the first guy James struck had a broken jaw but no one had life-threatening injuries. Two were at Cedars Sinai being interviewed by someone better than her.

James: 'I hope not. I really don't like hurting people. I just didn't want to get stomped.'

Mila: 'That's good. They teach us how to subdue people but not that. Anyway, we're following up on some threads but can't seem to collect any evidence against Chance or young Ed Harris.'

James: 'Christopher William Scott. I found out his name. I'm pretty sure he is the guy who shot Lauren.'

Mila: 'Ah, yes. We have spoken to Mr. Scott but he seems to have an alibi. He shot some scenes before and after the shooting and says he was in his trailer rehearsing in between. It is possible that he went out and came back but I don't have video of it.' Mila left off the part about hm being in 'Scrubs'.

Wondering about cameras on movie lots, James asked, 'Wouldn't they catch his car going out and coming in?'

Mila thought of this already. 'Yes but there is an office building and a few man doors around the lot where he could have went through that don't have security cameras.'

'I have Chance's phone records for the day. He was triangulated at home and took a lot of calls. We didn't think it was him in the parking lot so that checks out. So while I am inclined to believe you and Lauren, I am also wondering if there is anywhere else I should be looking or what I should be looking out for next.'

'I spoke with Kenneth and I'm glad he's keeping an eye on you guys.'

James, almost interrupting: 'You know Kenneth?'

Mila: 'Yeah, I know him. We've worked together in the past. He's solid. Oh, before I forget, why did you give your detail off this morning?'

It hit James that this is the real reason she called. She must have called Kenneth before calling him. Is he a suspect? As he thought about this, he realized he was taking too long to answer.

He blurted, 'They've been working around the clock for a while and part of the detail is up in Carmel with Lauren. I figured they needed a shift off. Besides, who attacks anyone at 7 o'clock in the morning?'

Mila's tone seemed to relax slightly. It was possible that she did it on purpose. 'Yeah, that is not normal.' She remained quiet, waiting for James to fill up the space with words.

James said, 'Well, that's all I know. Oh, I did call a private detective named Willie Bard, who said she would find out more about those people but I haven't heard back yet.'

'That won't be necessary. We are working on this so please don't interfere. And tell Kenneth to get his ass back to work,' Mila says and disconnects.

Up to this point, he wasn't sure that the LAPD was investigating but now knew that they were. The thought didn't give him comfort though; her question about dismissing the detail made the hairs on the back of his neck stand up. What the fuck? Was he a suspect? He didn't think so but he admittedly didn't know anything about police investigations.

He thinks for a minute and decides that he is definitely a suspect of some sort.

-

James called Lauren back and filled her in on the conversation with Mila. As he is telling her the story, he feels at home talking to her again. He entertained thoughts of Misty when Lauren pushed back on him but just talking to her reinforced his feelings for her. While he was very physically attracted to Misty, he had already made the connection with Lauren.

He was a little afraid of getting hurt again, but thought he was going to try to make it work. She was smart and funny, not just laughing at his jokes, but going with them and then making them funnier.

If Lauren stayed distant though, he could possibly cushion the blow with Misty. When he heard it in his head, he thought it sounded petty and immature, like something a kid would do. But he couldn't help thinking it anyway and thought that genetics might have something to do with it.

-

During Lauren's research, she found out that the evolution of homo sapiens from their more primitive roots had a major jump in progress around 7,000 years ago. Evolutionarily-speaking, that just happened.

So the fact that some of us are over-protective or jealous or feel the need to hunt/gather is not a foreign concept. We haven't had a tremendous amount of time to develop from our primitive, ancestral ways. In comparison to Homo Sapiens 50,000-year age, sharks are about 450 million years old. Lauren thinks that an alien intervention is not a very far-fetched concept, when you think about it.

So, she thought, how long has society had to develop compared to other animals? Not a long time at all. No wonder we're all fucked up.

19.

Chance found out later that same Monday from his bouncer friend about David Prince and his failed attempt to beat James up in the parking lot of his gym at seven in the goddam morning. He thinks about how bad of an idea that was until the bouncer tells him about the viral video of it. Even though it is only 1pm, Chance Baris believes he is going to need a drink to watch it.

He went to his glass-and-wood, mid-century modern bar in the living room and poured himself a crystal tumbler of Macallan 18, then sat on a stool and took out his phone. He searched 'Monterey Jones' and the let the video roll.

The first time Chance watched the clip, he thought it was sped up or spliced, like they used to do with old film. The guy on the left side of the frame was moving too fast and Monty was moving at normal speed. He watched it again, ignoring the Jason Bourne comment, as realized that everyone besides James on the left side frame was moving at Monty Jones speed also.

Chance gulped the 18-year-old scotch in his left hand. What kinda bullshit was that? he thought. Thoroughly rehearsed, choreographed movie fight scenes didn't land that well. While he was thinking that maybe someone was setting him up, a small window popped up and suggested the next reel, which was the security camera footage. He watched.

Setting his rage aside, Chance made a few phone calls, handling budget issues on a project with almost no budget and giving post-production direction on a much bigger project that was starting to run over. Another movie was released last weekend and doing surprisingly well. You never know what will land well with audiences.

He stews on it all week, the rage at his own inability to fix this bullshit building inside of him like the underground roiling of a volcano about to erupt.

On Friday, he is unable to concentrate and heads to the Katana at 7pm, staying on the bar floor most of the night, with Misty worriedly watching him from beneath camera 7. He was buzzed when he got there and never tapped the brakes, drinking more than she had ever seen. She wanted to give him drinks mixed with her water from her Chopin bottle but he was drinking scotch tonight.

At midnight, he headed to the office with a girl to do some lines of cocaine. Misty wasn't sure if they left and snuck into the back to find out, overhearing them in the office. She wished they had left because he might be trouble later. He had gotten into fights in his own nightclub before.

Misty returned to her spot at the bar. It was a little slow until a show at the Hollywood Bowl let out and then it was packed. At some point, she lost track of where Chance.

Back at Chance's house, Shannah, a tall, 27-year-old blonde actress, enjoys the view from the hot tub on the expansive rear deck overlooking Hollywood and the Los Angeles basin. She didn't have a swimsuit with her and is wearing her white lace bra and panties, which are see through when dry but were almost invisible when wet.

She moves over to Chance, wine in her left hand, and reaches for his shorts. He's not excited yet and Shannah sets her glass down and tries to get him going. When nothing happens, she makes fun of his cocaine-and/or-alcohol fueled inability to perform. He grabs her by the throat, which gets his equipment working, and gets rough with her.

He vaguely recalls going to the bedroom with her. The last thing he can remember is Shannah enjoying his performance but it is all very cloudy. When Chance wakes up in the morning, his guest does not.

He remembers snapshots of the night before. Him talking to two girls in somewhat conservative clothes and thinking they were bi and he had the opportunity to go to bed with both. Him dancing with a brunette in a microskirt. Coke on the desk. Drinking water(?) in the jacuzzi with a mostly naked brunette. Same brunette? Scotch again. His right hand around her throat, her face a mask of pleasure or pain, he wasn't sure which.

For someone who knows how to access the 'dark web' as he does, he knows there aren't neon billboards out there for hitmen or body removal services like movies insinuate. How do you get rid of a body? There are a hundred ways in books and movies, like a chipper or a furnace or weighing them down in the water, but none of those are available to him. And, for no apparent reason he can fathom, he has cartoon-like hate for fucking boats.

With no one else to call, he calls Billy for help. After Billy picks up, he says, 'Hey, I need your help with another thing. If you can help me with this production gig, I can double what I offered before.' Chance figures that this is a way to push things forward. Maybe Billy helps and earns his continued existence, maybe he goes away at the same time. Billy agrees and Chance says, 'Be here 10 minutes ago,' a line from 'Wild and Young' that he liked to use often.

Billy backs into Chance's gate in an old Nissan pickup truck, wearing dated jeans and a baseball cap. He's there for dirty work. Good, Chance thinks.

In the bed of the pickup is a large box attached to a pallet. Billy removes the straps holding the lid on the box and pitches the lid to the side. He's parked behind the date palms and no one can see what he is doing from the street.

'Where?' Billy asks. He doesn't say it is a she or a body and Chance thinks that this makes him weak. Chance, in his linen pants and button-up shirt, is the authority figure here and is dressed like it. Even though Billy is helping him, he wants Billy to remember the hierarchy here.

Billy takes a moving dolly out of the back seat of the truck and looks to Chance for direction. Chance leads him wordlessly into the house and the master bedroom, where the guest still is. Billy slides one end of her naked body off of the bed and onto the dolly, with the bulk of her weight on the wheels.

Chance is fascinated by the logical thinking on Billy's part. Where did he get the box on a pallet so quickly? How did he think of bringing wheels to move the body?

Billy rolls the blonde out to the back of the pickup truck and asks Chance for help picking her up, stating that if he put her in the box first, that they would have to lift the girl and the box. They lift the small-but-surprisingly-heavy girl into the truck and then into the box.

They put her clothes and shoes in the box also. Billy stops and opens her bag and fishes out her car keys.

'Here,' he says to Chance, handing him the keys and her phone and dropping her bag in the box. 'Drive over to the Katana with her phone and park your car. Put your phone on your desk and take her car to the closest Starbucks. Leave her phone in it and walk back. That way, your story is you drove her to the club and she left this morning. You stayed at work for a while.'

While Chance thinks this through, he notices that the pallet is strapped to the bed of the truck. Billy puts the top on the box and straps that down. To a causal observer, it looks like they are just moving some random merchandise in a pickup truck.

Chance is impressed with the speed and efficiency of Billy on this. And most of all, he is impressed with the forethought. He decides that he could expand this organization a little more and possibly put Billy in a management position, insulating himself.

Billy tells Chance that he'll take care of this part, pointing at the crate.

When Billy leaves, Chance quickly changes into something more comfortable for walking and hopped into his Maserati. He does exactly as Billy said, parks at the club, takes Shannah's Audi to Starbucks and walks a little over a mile back to the Blue Katana.

Billy drives the pallet containing someone's dead child north out to the back of an empty warehouse off of I5 in an area of warehouses in the middle of nowhere, some vacant, some active, during the day. He pulls behind an inactive warehouse with abandoned pallets and boxes piled high, the nearest fast-food restaurant a half mile away.

Billy unstraps the box from the truck bed, ties a rope to the pallet and around a large sprinkler pipe near the wall, buried in the trash. He steps hard on the gas and the box-pallet combo slides out of the bed of the truck and lands as it sat in the truck. Billy stops and gets out of the truck. He heads back to the pile with a bottle of campfire lighter fluid, thinking that he needs to get out of there.

He looked around to make sure no one was watching him. He didn't really look at her when he was at Chance's house, respecting the fact that this was Chance's girl, like they were dating. Partly because of that and partly because he didn't want Chance to think he was memorizing the damage.

But now, alone, his curiosity gets the better of him and he opens the box to really look at her.

Her hair is all over the place but he can see bruises on her neck. He moves her hair and sees that the left side of her face is a little bruised too, like as if she was slapped in the face a lot. He's afraid of seeing her eyes but thinks that she probably liked getting slapped around.

There are also bruises on her back and butt, the latter taking the brunt of the punishment. He pictures her bent over, taking it hard from behind, and gets very aroused.

He looks around again to see if he is still alone and sees cars getting on and off the freeway a good distance away. He wants to take care of himself there, on her maybe, if he drags her out of the box. Maybe put his fingers inside...

He feels a wave rush over him and realizes that he came in his pants. In a panic, pants smeared, he dumps lighter fluid on his pallet and a few others. He throws a stick match onto the box and walks back to the truck.

There is no 'whump' like in the movies, which Billy would like, but the effect is the same. Everything is on fire behind the empty warehouse by the time Billy gets on the ramp to I5 South back to LA.

He's stays turned on for the entire ride home.

20.

That Saturday, James gets an email from Willie Bard with information on Christopher William Scott and Chance Baris.

He reads through it, not finding a criminal record or police reports for either of them. There is a complaint by a woman named Cherice Growler against Chance that was dropped but it didn't say what the complaint was about. It could be that she didn't get paid for an acting gig or it could be rape.

It also contains anything that is a public record, like properties they own, as well as some personal information since they are both public figures somewhat. Well, that's no help, he thinks, he's still on his own.

-

James is alone on a Saturday night. He doesn't mind it normally and could usually find someone to hang out with or play games with online but when Lauren coming into his life, he realizes that he liked being with someone now. Almost like he was on hold. Having a girl in his life full time has made him want to go out more, to do more.

He wants to see a play and go to a museum but isn't going to that alone. James feels the need to be social, and mostly that happens in bars, so he decides to go out and see if he can meet up with some local friends.

He plans to hit the usual places, looking first into the large, folding, open windows of Sharkees. Since it is mainly an after-work happy hour place and today is Saturday, Sharkees is quiet.

Since it is still early, he changes his tactic and heads to a surfer bar along the strand. Since the surf has died down, there is a decent number of locals there eating shrimp tacos and having beers. He asks a few how the waves were, making small talk and having a few Modelos. He enjoys this crowd for a few reasons. They are almost always upbeat. They are never pretentious. And they always introduce hm a new slang term for 'good' or 'bad'.

Most folks in surf bars are in swimsuits and usually still wet, so they don't hang out long. As soon as dark comes, the bar empties and James calls an Uber.

He texts Lauren from the Uber to see how she is doing but gets no reply.

He goes to a bar called the Snake Pit and bumps into Matt, a guy he went to school with. They ran in different circles back then, but you could talk to anyone in a bar, really. They talked for a while, Matt talking about his current band and James asking questions. He promises to go see them at the Roxy in two weeks.

When the conversation dies down, he thinks about going to see Misty. He's told himself that he wants to talk to her about him possibly being a suspect. He might casually bring up the viral video of him, in case she hasn't seen it.

James was definitely not going to see Misty when he was sober but, with some drinks in him, it seemed like a good idea. Plus, who was going to say he couldn't? Lauren hadn't texted him back, but, checking his watch, realized that he sent the text only an hour ago.

He thought about how she pulled away from him. And he thought that, even though it was safer to be up in Carmel with her mom, she still kinda left him.

James told himself that he was overreacting, that he shouldn't be upset with her for pulling back or going up north. They just met recently and *moved in* together right away, which is not normal. So it *is* perfectly logical that they slow it down a little.

But he wasn't really interested in logic. She was probably going to end it once this was all over so who cares what he did.

After a few beers and some alone time, he was able to convince himself. He pulled up his Uber app. He finishes his third beer, drops a twenty-dollar tip on the bar and goes outside.

-

The night is warm. He checks the app as a car pulls to the curb and he gets in.

His detail is around him somewhere, keeping a loose but protective net around him. He's happy, no, more like satisfied, he thinks, that he can go out for drinks while being under some kind of threat and know that he won't get attacked.

He hasn't once thought about his wealth or what it can do for him in this way. He knows there is money and that his actual 'net worth' is high but he's not running around with a million in cash coming in every month. With so many apartments, so many mortgages, so much overhead, he feels more like a businessman with a decent paycheck more than wealthy. Far from wealthy.

The detail makes him feel, in his slightly inebriated state, important.

When he arrives at the Blue Katana, he hops out of the Uber and walks in. He notes a person getting out of the passenger seat of a car at a red curb and a motorcycle pulling up to a parking spot, noting that they are part of his detail.

He feels like he's rolling now. He has momentum.

When he gets up to the bar, Misty looks over and positively *beams* at him. In the short time that he's known her, James didn't think that she had ever looked like this before.

He glows on the inside when he sees her face, her excitement to see him. The feeling of making this beautiful woman, who seems to have embodied the 'Meh' emoji previously, excited to see *you* is powerful, exhilarating. Between the security detail, besting three thugs in a parking lot and her reaction, he feels more positive about himself than he ever has before.

It is all stroking his ego something fierce.

-

Unaware of what she looks like to the rest of the people here, Misty runs over to James and leans over the bar to kiss him. He leans up and she kisses him on the lips. She's happier than she thought she would be to see him and feels a confidence at his arrival that her feelings are somewhat reciprocated.

He looks good in his dark jeans and the black t-shirt that fits well on his muscular arms and shoulders. Misty stupidly feels underdressed for a second but realizes that she's wearing dark pants and a black, well-fitted shirt also. She means to tell him 'good to see you' but says, 'I'm happy you came to see me,' instead. She's a little embarrassed but James is quick to ease her.

She is wearing a black see-through shirt with a black bra on underneath and yoga pants with side pockets for her phone and bottle opener. Feeling a little self-conscious, she adjusts her shirt.

-

He looks at her, his eyes going from her face and moving down as far as he can with the bar in the way, looks back up at her face and, smiling, says, 'My God, who wouldn't want to see *you*.'

Misty turns pink, turns and walks down the bar to get him a beer, a little strut in her step. He watches and waits, and when she returns with the open bottle and pint glass, he says, 'Do a shot with me.'

Normally she would have a shot from the water/Chopin bottle but that is not going to do it today. They do two shots of chilled Grey Goose vodka with lemon backers, smiling at each other.

Misty heads down the bar to help some other people and James sips his beer, feeling the eyes of guys on him, all al little jealous of his status with Misty. He absorbs it but doesn't revel in it. It's not something he enjoys, making others feel bad or jealous.

He feels like the edges of the past few weeks or months have rounded off and maybe have calmed down a little.

-

When she has a minute, Misty walks back over to James and says, 'So, what's happening with the whole, you know, craziness?'

James replies, 'Well, Lauren left, the cops think I'm a suspect or something and I got jumped outside the gym at 7am.'

'What?!,' Misty says, 'When was this?'

'I got jumped Monday,' James says. 'I'm surprised you didn't see it on Insta.'

'It's VIRAL?' she half shouts.

James pulls his personal phone and opens his saved videos on Instagram. He hands the phone to Misty.

Misty takes it, watching Monty Jones' abs, then booty for a second, wondering if he showed her the wrong thing. Then she sees it on the left side of the screen. A blur of a human moving through large people, taking them down with amazing speed. Her jaw involuntarily drops when she realizes it's him and scrolls back to the beginning of the video.

She thinks, I knew from him throwing Billy that he was good but what in the fuck is this. It looks fake but really good, like when Jason Bourne kills another assassin with a pen or a book but those scenes are shot close up and cut a lot to be more impressive. She scrolls back and watches it again. She was right before, he's a superhero but doesn't know it.

She hands him back his phone and says, 'I'm happy that you didn't get hurt. But, you know, I'm probably not going to worry about you so much after this.' She puts her folded forearms on the bar, leans in and looks into his eyes. 'That video is fucking hot as hell,' she says, unblinking. 'And I'm not talking about that girl's ass.'

James blushes at that, but recovers quickly and says, 'Wait, there's a girl's ass in that video?'

'So you're a suspect now?' Misty asks. She was going to ask about Lauren leaving but went this way instead. It was like mentioning her name might ruin what was happening with her and James.

'Yeah, the detective called and asked me a bunch of questions. I don't get it. How would I save someone from a kidnapping but be the kidnapper?'

Misty said, 'You could have staged the kidnapping attempt. You could be working with Billy.'

James: 'Kidnapping someone I had never met, or seen, before? That doesn't track.'

Misty: 'That's not necessarily true. You could have been stalking her for months, peeking through bushes or having her followed. I think it is easy to put a tracker on a car now.'

James: 'I didn't know you were the romantic type.'

Misty laughs out loud, mouth open, showing off her earth shattering smile at the end. 'Yeah, no. I have never been accused of that before.'

He stays with her until closing, sipping on beers slowly as to not be sloppy. They talk less when the club is busy, more when its slow, but regularly making eye contact with each other throughout the night. Sideways smiles, coy glances.

He stays inside while she and the rest of the staff clean up, volunteering to help out or to take off if he's in the way. They assure him that he's good and he stays.

At 2:45, Misty says goodbye to her coworkers and says to James, 'Let's go hang out.'

James, always thoughtful, asks, 'Are you hungry?'

Misty: 'Nah. I might be hungry in like an hour or so but never hungry right after work. I could use a drink though.'

James: ‘Nothing is open but we can hang out at my place. I don’t have a car so you might have to drive...’

After seeing his Aston Martin, Misty did NOT want James to see her ratty old Civic. ‘I didn’t drive today,’ she says when they get outside, maybe fifty feet from her car, which sits camouflaged in a pile of other cars owned by the staff.

James pulls his phone and requests an Uber, making his destination the Hermosa Beach house. He asks, ‘So how did you do tonight?’

She replies, ‘I made $245 in cash tips. We don’t know how much in credit card tips until tomorrow.’

He’s not sure if that is good or not but assumes it is and says, ‘Oh nice.’

She thinks it could have been worse, especially because she knows James left a $200 tip on his credit card bill. As she is about to say something, the Uber shows up and saves them from further tip conversations.

Misty sees the motorcycle guy and the guy-and-girl in the car near the curb while she was getting in the Uber but doesn’t know that they are James’ detail. She remembers what James said about being a suspect and thinks they might be cops. Usually when she gets out of work, no one is around.

When they get in the car, James types quickly into his phone and puts it away. Misty suspects that it might be a text to Lauren, not knowing that James typed ‘Hermosa’ and sent it to Kenny. She decides that she will make sure he has no more thoughts about Lauren tonight...

‘So, what do you do for a living,’ she asks, scootching closer in the back of the car.

James’ standard response is Developer or Property Manager, but he says, ‘My company owns some properties.’ Misty thinks that really means that James owns properties. No one drives an Aston Martin that isn’t rich. ‘What kind of properties?’

‘Apartment buildings, rental houses. That’s all pretty boring. I get to develop land into houses sometimes, which is fun.’

'Oh cool,' Misty says, keeping the attention on James. 'What's your favorite project so far?'

James thinks for a minute and says, 'There was this old house I found in between some mountains at the top of La Crescenta-Montrose. The house and an old stable were abandoned for years, both completely falling down. I rebuilt the house, adding a second floor and a wrap-around porch and a paddock, rebuilt the stable and added a barn.'

Misty thought about the question she was going to ask, and finally said, 'James, what's a paddock?' She's pretty sure she knew what it was since there were horse properties on the outskirts of Fresno but thought the question would make him feel smarter.

'Oh,' James paused, 'it's like an open area for horses to run around.'

The Uber pulls up near the ivy-covered staircase and they get out, thanking the driver, who was on the phone with someone for the whole ride.

'Someone must love that guy. Who is he talking to at 3am?' James asks.

Misty thinks about that and realizes that no one has really cared about her in a long time. She checks in with her mom once every week or two but they're both pretty busy. Misty thinks that maybe her mom feels kinda guilty about what happened to their family and might be avoiding her some of the time.

She doesn't want to drive an Uber or anything but at that moment she's jealous of their driver.

James heads up the stairs first, Misty in tow, not really noting the detail pulling up and taking positions around the house.

-

When they get upstairs, James asks Misty what she would like to drink. 'Vodka and anything,' she says, and James pulls a can of something from the fridge and makes his way to a bar between the sliding glass doors. Misty walks over to the closest doors, opens one and walks out onto a balcony where she can hear the waves crashing.

The onshore breeze is cold and she shivers for a second before James shows up behind her with a chunky throw and a drink.

Even though she can only see streetlights from the strand and a reflection of the moon on the ocean, the sound of the waves crashing, the view and salty air are wonderful to her. She smiles deeply when she takes the throw over her shoulders and drink in her hand.

It is this moment in her life that she realizes that she will never live in Fresno again. She believes that she will refer to this exact point in time as the pivotal moment where you know that there is no going back.

She turns her face up to him and gently kisses him on the cheek. 'Thank you,' she says softly. She's not thinking of what to do next or how this will move her forward or really anything else at that point, only living in the moment for possibly the first time in her life. She's content hearing the waves crash, the sound calming her whole body completely. She loves the warm blanket on her body with the cool breeze on her face, thinking that the balance of these two things may hold the meaning of life.

When she takes her first sip of her drink, she finishes about seventy-five percent of the contents of her glass. She regrets it for a split second, thinking she's done too much, that she will all-of-a-sudden blurt out her actual age or whatever but she doesn't need to fill up this space with words.

James says, 'Come this way,' and leads her around to a wooden outdoor staircase she hadn't seen before. They go up.

On the roof is a gazebo with a hot tub, bar and a TV. One side is open towards the sea, with the roll-up shades on the other three sides closed.

They stop just outside of it for a few seconds and take in the view.

There are heaters glowing around the upper perimeter of the structure. James goes behind the bar to make drinks, while Misty takes off her pants and shirt. James stops his mixing and watches her step into the hot tub in her matching plain gray bra and underwear.

There is a vague pang in the back of his brain but, as he watches her step into the hot tub, it goes away quickly enough. James thinks quickly about what he's wearing under his pants and realizes that he is wearing his new, red boxer briefs.

'When did you put the heaters on?' Misty asks.

'I opened an app while I was making the drinks downstairs...'

He puts the drinks on the edge of the hot tub and takes off his pants and shirt. Tightening his abs as hard as possible to brace himself against the initial shock of water, he steps in, handing Misty her vodka-and-something, and submerging most of himself in one corner.

She takes the drink from him thinking she needs to let go of something...

-

Misty watched her parents split and her family fall apart, which was a pivotal moment in her life. She doesn't understand that the experience shaped the way she thinks, that she has become a person who feels like they need to control every aspect of their life. She needs to make sure that doesn't happen to her again, even though, on a deeper level, she somewhat understands control is an illusion.

-

James, noticing that she was staring off into the distance a bit but oblivious as to what is happening inside Misty's head, says, 'Is it hot enough?'

Misty, refocusing her attention, her gratitude to him for showing her this, says, 'This is wonderful. Thank you for bringing me here,' moves into the middle of the hot tub and kisses him on the lips.

James runs his hands over her small frame. Youth, alcohol and virility take over, with neither James nor Misty having the ability to stop it.

-

On Sunday morning, James wakes up to find himself naked against Misty's slight but shapely frame, her hair draped across his chest. He didn't realize that she had so much hair and he quickly thinks of her like a doll from the Trolls movies.

He's not sure if she s awake too, his bedroom being mostly dark with light peeking out from behind the blackout curtains.

Misty has been awake, thinking, for a while. She's thinking that, if this was going to be a relationship, she doesn't really have anything to offer this guy. She doesn't have money or a great job, she's from a not-so-great area and, while she is in good shape now, she may not always be. She thinks about how she can change that.

But first, she wants to make sure that Lauren doesn't come back into the picture.

'I don't want to get up,' Misty says unexpectedly. 'Can we just stay right here for a while?'

James was lost in thought, thinking about the sex the night before and was getting turned on while he thought about it. Unlike other girls, Misty did whatever she wanted to James. In the hot tub, rinsing off in the shower and (mostly) on the bed. While he was taking a short break in between rounds, she played with herself, putting his fingers in her mouth and putting her mouth on him while she did it. It was hot.

She wasn't subtle. Not exactly aggressive but close to it. Like she *needed* it. *Needed* him. She encouraged him to pull her hair, to go harder.

'Oh,' Misty said without moving from her small spoon position, 'it seems that you are already, uh, up.'

-

Afterward, she got James to talk about himself more while they showered and dressed, asking questions about his childhood, upbringing and school. She showered with the door open, got dressed slowly in front of him.

James asked if she wanted to go to Starbucks but Misty declined, saying she would just have coffee at his house, if he had some. She has things to do early (for her) today. He made them coffee and offered to drive her home, and she accepted.

Since the Rivian was at the Santa Monica house, James took her in the Aston Martin. They did not bring their coffee into the Aston Martin.

On the ride, she said that she didn't work on Sundays, which was the only day she didn't work, and would like to see him later if he was around. Although a little worn out from the night before, James wanted to see her again and agreed.

That was before the guilt kicked in.

21.

Billy received a call from someone named Danny on Sunday, asking him questions like his social security number and address, bank information and tax status. It turns out that Chance is putting Billy on the production company's payroll for $175,000 a year.

This is a total score for him, having a guaranteed salary for the first time since waiting tables. He felt like his luck had taken a turn for the better and knew it was smart to keep friends like Chance.

-

Misty gets home and texts her friend Suki and asks for a ride to the club so she could get her car. While she did leave with James, she didn't necessarily want everyone to know that she spent the night with him. Since she had never left with anyone from the club before, it would be believable that maybe she didn't spend the night.

She throws clothes into one of the washing machines in the tiny common laundry area of her small apartment complex and gets changed. Suki, a bartender from the Yeti that she had a short and purely physical relationship with, picks her up and runs her to the club to get her car.

Misty thanks her and kisses her on the lips, which goes a little longer than expected, getting Misty to think.

'What are you doing later?' she asks Suki.

Suki smiles and says playfully, 'What did you have in mind?'

'Well,' Misty says slowly, 'I have this new friend...'

-

Misty texts James' personal phone in the early afternoon, asking him if he wants to meet for drinks at Casa de Castro, a popular Mexican restaurant with warm bean dip and great margaritas.

James, who has been feeling guilty about Lauren, realizes that she hasn't texted him back from last night, and writes back, 'Shure'.

Castros, as it is known among Angelenos, is very popular on Friday afternoons and Sunday brunches. When James arrives, it is 4:30 and the place is quiet with only a few tables outside taken.

The hostess is expecting him and leads him from the entrance. Misty is there already, in a booth near the open patio doors, with a taller Asian girl that could be a model.

James introduces himself and puts a hand out to shake. Suki uses it to pull him closer, purses her lips, leans to kiss him and James puckers. She kisses him on both cheeks and says, 'Hi, I'm Suki,' in a French accent. She's wearing what looks to be a blue linen skirt and a white linen top, the clothes barely clinging on to her small frame.

'Nice to meet you too,' James says and slides into the booth next to Misty.

He notices that there are three margaritas on the table, one full and two missing some, all on the rocks with salt on the rims. These are not blended drink girls, he guesses. He doesn't notice Suki looking him over.

Feeling guilty about Lauren, James thought about ending it today when he left the house to meet Misty. He was on the fence about it, not sure what to do.

'How do you two know each other?' James starts the conversation.

The day is warm and sunny. Misty, looking more casual than usual in a skirt and top, is animated more than usual as well. She tells James that they interviewed at the Katana on the same day but Suki took a job at the Yeti before Chance could call her. Suki added in that she thought Chance was creepy and wouldn't have taken the job there anyway.

He sips his margarita. It is delicious. They seem to know everyone on staff at Castros and more margaritas and food come out without them placing orders.

During the conversation, James notices that Misty smiles and touches Suki a lot, which James hadn't seen before. He hadn't actually seen her physically touch anyone but him, starting after the fight with Billy. He had thought maybe she only touches people she's attracted... Oh. That is when it hits him.

Suki puts her hand high up on Misty's thigh when she leans over to talk to James.

He sips his margarita a little harder, feeling the tequila in this one. He notices that they might be wearing bikinis under their clothes. James stops thinking about what might happen and starts thinking about what to do next.

After the nachos have been ravaged, Suki gets up to use the restroom. When she's out of sight, even though he doesn't want to kill the fun vibe happening, James leans to Misty and says, 'If you brought her here to get me to like you more, you didn't have to. I already like you.'

Misty puts her head down for a second, looking very young. After a moment, she picks her head up and says, 'Well, I'm not rich or a doctor or anything so I thought I might make it more interesting for you. Do you want me to ask her to leave?'

Quickly, and in a serious tone, James says, 'You don't have to be anything but who you are. And no, she'll be heartbroken if she can't come hang out with us. Poor thing. We have to think about her too.'

Misty laughs and leans over to James, kissing him and putting her arms around his neck. Suki comes back while they are kissing, slides in up against James on his side of the booth, puts her hand on his upper thigh and says, 'This is nice.'

They don't get a bill from Casa de Castro so James leaves two one-hundred-dollar bills on the table as a tip. They decide to spend the rest of the day doing fun things around LA.

Even though James' Aston Martin Vantage doesn't have back seats, they take his car. Suki sits in the passenger seat with Misty on her lap, Suki announcing that she is going to be 'all hands' in the car.

They go to an upscale cocktail bar in downtown LA where the girls get frothy muddled drinks and James gets a beer. The girls don't usually order frothy muddled drinks because of the length of time and effort that go into them but they're doing something different today.

Then they head to Koreatown and go to a karaoke place with individual rooms, where they order bottle service and close the blinds.

By popular vote, James sings first. He picks a fun song that he can almost sing and the girls help with backing vocals. Misty is up second, singing 'Don't Stop Believing' by Journey, which is pretty good, with Suki and James helping on the chorus.

Suki sings an Adele song so well that James doesn't believe it is her at first and moves the microphone away from her face. With looks like that and an incredible voice, how is she not the biggest celebrity in the world?

Afterward, they head to the Hermosa house for a quick dip in the ocean and a longer dip in the hot tub. The girls do have on bikinis underneath their clothes but James has to change for the beach. He leaves them in the kitchen with bottles of water and the open bar.

They make drinks and Misty shows Suki around a little, taking her onto the balcony to watch the sun start setting, but not up to the roof yet.

-

After a quick dip in the ocean, they go through a gate in between houses to an outdoor shower to rinse off and grab some towels from a cubby in the wall next to it. They head to the roof to catch the last of the sunset from the hot tub.

They drink water to keep from dehydrating in the hot water and then follow up with tequila drinks. James notes that they were drinking tequila all day and didn't mix in vodka or wine. They also seemed a little tipsy but not hammered.

Suki pulled out a pack of cigarettes from her bag and looked a question to James, who nods and says, 'Enjoy.' She lit it, took a drag and blew out smoke. With her other hand, she reached behind herself and untied her bikini top, tossing it into the corner of the gazebo.

They sit in the hot tub for 30 minutes watching the sunset and chatting, with Suki and Misty tell stories of bar shenanigans. When it is full dark, they head downstairs. Once inside, James goes to the fridge and asks if anyone is hungry. He turns around check their reaction to food, only to see Misty and Suki kissing, pawing at each other's bikinis.

'I'm gonna go with 'no', he says, and pulls them down the hallway to his bedroom.

-

On Monday, Billy arrives on set early, as usual. Also, as usual, he heads over to Craft Services for coffee and something to eat. He usually gets a pastry and a protein bar. But today is unusual. The usual folks at Craft Services are not there. Instead of the nice, fifty-something woman with the gray streaks in her hair, there is a girl.

The girl is possibly in her twenties, of Latin heritage, and pretty. He thinks possibly in her twenties because about fifty percent of Latinas that he has met and thinks are twenty are actually thirty-five. He's pretty sure they don't age until they're like fifty or so.

She's short, maybe 5'2", with long, dark brown hair. He thinks her 5'2" is a perfect match to his 5'8".

She smiles at him. Her brown eyes twinkle. She has strong, runner's thighs, which are a little thicker than a lot of LA girls, and a flat stomach.

While he would often grunt a 'hnnh' at the forty-something, he's momentarily thrown off of his routine and says 'Hi'. Still smiling but looking either shy or embarrassed, she nods at him and he assumes that she doesn't speak much English.

He's still riding the high of getting a fixed salary from Chance and tries his luck.

'Primero dia?' he asks. Upon arriving in LA, Billy realized that there is a large population of Spanish speaking people here so he figured it would be smart to learn it. Despite his conservative political leanings, Latinas are hot. Billy thinks that his brain may lean one way or another, but his dick isn't prejudice at all.

'At this job, yes,' she replies in perfect English, 'but it's not my first job. What can I help you with?' He pauses, the English reply was not what he expected.

He smiles before he says, 'I wasn't trying to insult you by speaking Spanish, just trying to make you feel comfortable in a place I thought was new for you.'

She replies, 'No estaba seguro de cuánto Espanol entiendes,' wondering how much he will get.

Billy answers in English, 'I understood most of what you said.'

She appreciates that he tried to speak Spanish, that he tried to make her feel comfortable at a new job. She thinks he's cute and that he might be a decent person inside. Hard to tell with actors.

Billy turns slightly red and somewhat shy when he asks her, 'Hey so can I ask you out on a date? I'd love to take you to a play.. But I guess I might have to know your name first...'

'Lina,' she replies, liking the fact that this white guy actor who makes millions of dollars a year is asking her out. 'My name is Alina but my little brother could only say Lina, so it stuck.'

'We suck at poetry in America,' Billy adds, not thinking that Central and South America are actually Americas also, 'so much that we don't use beautiful names like Alina. We're so retarded that we re-hash names like Ingrid and Harriet. Why do we punish our children at birth?'

Lina liked the compliment but thought that he probably shouldn't use 'retarded' anymore. She almost declines his offer because of it but she likes how he turned shy when he was asking her out.

She says, 'I don't know that but I would like to see a play,' and smiles at him.

Billy's mind was straying a little, thinking about naming children Ingrid when her words sink in. He turns back to her and falls into her big brown eyes. 'Oh, that's cool. Now I guess I'll need your number too.'

Lina playfully puts her hand out, palm up. 'Phone.'

Billy reaches into his front pocket and hopes he didn't leave porn open on his phone last night. When he pulls it free, he unlocks it and quickly checks his open apps and doesn't see anything offensive. Satisfied that there isn't anything, he hands it to her.

She opens the messaging app and types in her number. She asks, 'What is your name?' When he answers, she types, 'Hi Alina, I'm Bill,' and hits send, sending herself a message from his phone. When she hands him his phone back, hers dings in her back pocket.

At this point, Billy does not remember what he was doing before he started talking to her. He smells coffee, which jars him back to his home planet, and says, 'Okay, I'll get us some coffee. I mean tickets. I'll find a show.' Alina smiles and chuckles, covering her mouth with her hand.

He gets coffee and grabs the closest shrink-wrapped muffin, swipes his card and says, 'Gracias, mucho gusto.'

Lina replies, 'Nice to meet you too, Bill.'

-

Normally when Billy gets a great role or some kind of positive in his life, he celebrates by going out and getting completely hammered. Maybe he picks up a girl and gets laid, maybe not. Today though, he doesn't want that at all.

He has a good part in a good movie, even though his part ends soon. But he also has a great salary and possibly a new girlfriend, which is amazing.

Growing up believing that he's not worthy of success or love, Billy has always been his own worst enemy. When he has gotten great parts with legendary directors, he's found a way to feel shame that he didn't get something right or that he wasn't enough to get a starring role from them later on. He's found ways to blame himself for his good-but-not-great income.

So while on set today, with his new-found income and his upcoming date, his outlook on life is shifting. For once, maybe it doesn't suck to be him.

21.

Lauren arrives two days later, James picking her up from the airport in the Rivian. They hug for a beat longer than most people at the airport curb do, inciting the police officer chasing waiting cars to light-heartedly comment 'Get a room'. They all chuckle, James kissing her head before releasing her to climb in the car.

Kenny informed James that there were some unmarked police cars floating around at various times and they all thought it might be okay to head back to Hermosa in the next few days. They make a plan to do just that.

-

Chance gets a text from an unknown number, which is not out of the ordinary for him. With his businesses, he deals with a lot of new people and doesn't store anyone's number if he thinks they're not important.

The message says, 'Lauren will be alone at 1134 Rivas Canyon Rd. in Santa Monica in one hour'. That would be at around 9pm.

He sends a message to Billy to see if he is around to go there but doesn't get a response. He decides that this is an opportunity that he won't pass up. Chance doesn't know who sent the text but knows that it would take about 40 minutes to get there. He puts on dark blue jeans and a black T shirt, grabs his Smith and Wesson .40 revolver and gets in the car.

-

James gets back to the Santa Monica house with Lauren and makes sure the detail is around. They talk a lot about everything, sitting in the yard on the lounge chairs that have finally arrived, in the kitchen and on the big sofa. They're talking about the future mostly, which is new for them.

Lauren doesn't know how to tell James her news. Every part of her wants to be there, to be with him, right now. Almost every part. There is a small part that thinks this is a mistake, that she should back off, that backing off will make things easier. But most of her wants to feel his hugs, to laugh out loud at the funny-nerdy way he does things. It feels *good* to laugh like that.

Her news is devastating though.

James uses the first-floor restroom and Lauren stands, walking around by the windows, looking at the pool. She's ready for bed and is pacing slightly, thinking she might be nervous about going to bed with James again.

-

Chance drives up through the open gate and right up to the front of the house. It looks like it was just renovated, judging by the staked trees close to the house and new-looking paint. He tries the front door and it is unlocked so he walks in.

He sees Lauren standing in front of a lot large glass windows, pool lit behind her, water-lit reflections bouncing around the ceiling. Chance thinks that whoever sent the text fucking nailed it. When Lauren sees Chance, she looks to her right quickly at a closed door, just as James steps out.

Chance gets the feeling that something is wrong and pulls the Smith and Wesson from the front left side of his waistband with his right hand. As he brings the gun around, James bolts toward Lauren with incredible speed, moving as if to tackle her. Lauren spins away from James as if to run into the kitchen. Since Chance doesn't have a lot of experience with guns, he yanks the trigger hard, pulling the gun up as he does it.

The windows behind James and Lauren shatter at the gun explodes, bullets hitting first behind James, then between he and Lauren, then in front of Lauren, each shot breaking through and shattering a different pane of tempered glass.

As is typical of most glass windows and doors made after 1970, the windows are double pane and tempered, the glass falling out in small pieces rather than large shards that could impale someone.

James reaches Lauren before shot number three, putting himself between her and Chance, herding her very quickly toward the kitchen as the third window shatters. Left arm around Lauren, he puts out his right fist like Superman and punches through the double broken panes as a shot hits low through another pane of glass near the kitchen.

James dives with Lauren into the pool as Chance's fifth and last shot sails out through an already-broken pane of glass, into the night, toward the Pacific Ocean. He yanks the trigger two more times before the click registers. He didn't bring additional ammunition and thinks, even though he's in the pool right now, that James can and would kick the living shit out of him if he stuck around.

He turns and runs back out through the front door and towards his car.

-

Jamal, on patrol on the downhill side below the house, hears the shots and scales the stone wall up to the pool with a quickness and agility that someone that big should not have. As he hops over the fence, he pulls his Colt 1911 from a leg holster and runs toward the broken glass, near where James and Lauren are in the water.

He scans for a target and glimpses the back of Chance through the open front door running to his car. He checks in with James and Lauren to see if they are okay, gets a yes, and stays in his shooting stance with his gun pointed toward the door in case the shooter is coming back in. He hears a car start with a loud rumble and follows the sound as it takes off through the open gate and down through the canyon. Maserati, judging by the distinctive sound.

Jamal doesn't take a shot at the person fleeing or give chase. That is not Jamal's job. His job is to protect people, these people, which is what he does. Although he highly doubts it, there could be more shooters in Maseratis waiting out front.

-

Chance thinks about what he should do next. His first thought is that he should go somewhere public so people see him somewhere. But where? Like a bar? Nah, that's stupid.

He thinks he'll need a solid alibi so he plans to call Billy or Misty and invite them over. Or both. Two people would be better. Billy can say that he got there at 8 and Misty a little later.

Fuck, he brought his phone. They might be able to track where his phone was. Nothing he could do about that now but thinks that he shouldn't make any calls just yet. He's not sure, but they might not have his location unless he makes a call.

When he gets home, he hits a button on the visor of his Maserati and the gate slides open. He dumps the car in front of the garage doors and heads inside to pour himself a scotch.

-

James calls Kenny from his work phone while his personal one sits wet on the counter. He is wishing he had some rice to put the phone in but doesn't. Lauren went to get changed and check her small bandages but thinks she's okay. Kenny calls Mila and a small army of police show up at the Santa Monica house on Rivas Canyon.

Detective Mila asks everyone a lot of questions for an hour before James realizes that Edgar had installed the security system for him over the weekend. He calls Edgar to come and pull the footage but Edgar is already there, coming up from the garage unexpectedly and startling a few officers.

They don't have to scrub too far to see the footage of Chance's arrival and hurried exit. Mila and a small team leave the rest of the cops there, just as the crime scene folks show up.

-

Billy gets a text from an unknown number that says, 'Be here 10 minutes ago' and says to the empty house, 'I guess Chance got a burner.' He's a little drunk, opting to stay home and have a couple of drinks and watch movies, as actors do. He puts on his shoes and goes to his car.

Chance's house is only 10 minutes away so he's not too worried about getting arrested for drinking and driving.

About halfway there, he realizes that he is wearing his slippers, which have a thin sole on them, because they keep slipping off when he is driving.

When he shows up at Chance's house, he sees that the gate is open and assumes Chance left it that way for him. When he walks up to the house, he sees that the front door is open a crack so he walks in, figuring the boss left it open so Billy doesn't have to ring the bell. As he does, he almost falls over Chance, who is laying in a pool of blood near the front door. Billy doesn't panic, maybe due to the alcohol, but turns and doesn't waste time. He gets right back into his car and drives back down the hill toward his house, tacking a small amount of Chance's blood with him.

Not knowing what to do, he sends Misty a text and asks if she has seen Chance lately. He wasn't sure if they could track a cell phone from tower to tower if it was texting or on a call but he thought that might be movie stuff. He thought that this looked like a movie style setup though and that maybe Misty could provide him an alibi.

Who would set him up? That kid James? James left a message with Misty to warn him off, she said. While James was fast and could fight, he didn't seem like a killer. James could have tried to hurt Billy during their fight but didn't. He had no idea who shot Chance and thought that he needs to keep himself off of the suspect list. He knew people were convicted with much less evidence in this country.

He thought about losing his new salary and screamed at the windshield, 'FUCK!' at the top of his lungs. He was planning on getting rid of this shitty BMW and buying himself something new for his date with Alina.

Misty doesn't text him back so he drives home, thinking he would just be sitting on his couch half drunk when the cops showed up. They wouldn't think he did it.

Billy walks in and sees the TV is still on the movie he was watching and his drink still has ice in it. He plops down on the couch, tips the rest of the contents of the glass into his mouth and tries to act like nothing happened, picking up the remote to scroll back to where he was when he left. But it was paused. He thought, wait, did I pause it?

20.

When Detective Mila and the two patrol cars arrive at Chance's house, they find him right away since the gate and front door are open and he is laying in the front doorway. She sarcastically says to the other cops, 'My detective training paid off, I found him.' Only some of the cops chuckle but they all pull their guns.

They do a quick search the house, which takes a while, and when they don't find anyone lying in wait, go take a look at Chance.

Once in the chest, once in the head. Like a professional. The blood is starting to dry a little around the edges and, although she's not a forensics expert, Mila's thought is that someone shot him the minute he got here. Or they got here. Was he with someone at Rivas Canyon?

-

Detective Mila Briçianos' most likely suspect in the murder of Chance Baris was James Willis but James was home with Parker, a security detail and cameras. Cameras, she thought again, and looked around the front of Chance's house. There they were, two cameras pointing somewhat at the entry. She'd have to wait until Crime Scene got there, which wouldn't be easy. Things were moving fast and she needed to stay on it.

When the Crime Scene folks arrived, they checked Chance's phone for fingerprints and looked at his right hand for defensive wounds or something under his fingernails. When she was cleared, they handed her a pair of latex gloves and she unlocked Chance's phone. In it was a password keeper, which was also unlocked with his fingerprint.

While she was doing that, a detective found the security room on the second floor, which looked like a walk-in closet. She went in and accessed the computer with a password from the phone, sending the cops to find a safe or some evidence, like a gun. She found footage of Christopher William Scott arriving and leaving Chance's house. She scrubbed before that, looking for Chance's arrival and not finding it, only a nineteen-minute gap in the time stamp. So Chance had had time to erase the video of himself coming home.

Why would he do that? Maybe he didn't.

-

While Mila was opening the safe in Chance's office, some cops arrived at Christopher William Scott's house in Los Feliz and found him on his couch, his Apple TV showing screen saver satellite pictures, a bullet wound in his right temple. The cops also found what looked like a bullet hole in the wall on the side of his TV, like he fired the gun before shooting himself. Was he testing the gun to make sure it worked? He should have known it worked if he just shot Baris.

The Crime Scene people were going to be busy today.

21.

Mila went through it again.

The running theory was that Chance went to Santa Monica to kill Lauren, judging by the deleted text from his phone providing the address, which failed. When Chance gets home, Christopher (Billy) shoots him and goes home and kills himself.

There were quite a few things that didn't add up with this though. Big holes in the theory. Who sent the text to Chance with the address? Why would Billy kill Chance?

There were two different guns, the no-number 9mm that killed Scott and Baris and the .40 cal that Baris used to shoot at Willis and Parker in the Santa Monica but the .40 was nowhere to be found. Did Scott toss it away on the way home to kill himself? Holes.

From the video, it didn't look like Scott had a gun when he arrived, or left, Chance's house. There is no direct footage of the front door but his hands look empty on the recordings they do have of the courtyard. Holes.

It was now likely that the theory of Baris having some obsession with Lauren was correct and that he sent Scott to kidnap her then shoot her. They were still looking for Tony the bouncer from the kidnapping attempt but not having any luck.

The 9mm was, at one point in its life, fitted with a silencer. Where was the silencer?

As for motive, who would kill Baris and Scott? The most likely suspect in the killing of Chance Baris now would be Misty McCarthy, since, according to the documents in Baris's safe, she was set to inherit everything he had. House, cash, production company, royalties, everything. Baris's father was in a home for memory loss and was provided for in the documents.

But that didn't explain why Scott died or how she became the inheritor.

As for opportunity, McCarthy was placed at the Blue Katana around the time of the killings, according to her colleague, Mike Zuniga. Zuniga confirmed that she was there and that she closed up, just like she does the other 5 nights a week. She took a break to get some food but she did that every night also. Zuniga said she was gone for about 30 minutes. Holes.

The cameras were not working at the club for about a week prior to the events, he added.

She didn't send anyone to the Blue Katana on the night of the murders. By the time they had gotten through the paperwork in Chance's vault, it was 2:30am and most of the cops were on overtime. So, they waited until the next morning to talk to Zuniga and McCarthy.

-

James texted Misty at around 1am, after the police left, but she didn't text back. He figured since she was at work that she must be busy.

James and Lauren went to the Hermosa Beach house, seeing as the Santa Monica house had a breeze running through it.

-

As she works nights, Detective Mila and a uniformed officer woke Misty up when they arrived at her apartment early the next morning. They asked her where she was last night, about her relationship with Chance Baris and if she new a Lauren Parker.

She said that she was at work last night and that Mikey (Zuniga) could confirm that. Inviting them in, Misty said that she had a physical relationship with Chance on occasion but he wasn't introducing her to his mother or anything. They weren't serious.

She said she knew Lauren peripherally, that she was a customer that came in with her friend Holly. She asked what happened and Detective Mila told her that Chance and Christopher William Scott had been killed.

Still standing in her small living/dining room, Misty put her hand to her mouth and asked, 'Was it drugs?'

Mila asked, 'What makes you say that?'

Misty said, 'Well, it's a nightclub. I know they did drugs sometimes but I don't know if they were dealing it. Like, you know, a lot of it. I never see drug dealers in the club so I wondered if they were like, truck-load people.'

'Have you seen trucks with drugs in them?' Mila asked.

'No,' Misty, in her pajamas, said, 'but, you know, who would send a truckload of drugs to a nightclub? But Chance always had a gun and cash.'

'What kind of drugs did they do?' Mila asked.

'Cocaine. I didn't see anything else, come to think of it.'

Mila took a mental note to look into a drug angle and needed to get a team to search Chance's office at the nightclub. It should have been done last night but too late for that now.

Misty was going to ask if she needed to call her lawyer but thought that these questions weren't about her, really, so she left it alone.

Detective Mila, on 4 hours of sleep, said she would be back in touch soon.

-

Elizabeth Crawley worked with Chance Baris on a few occasions. She helped him set up a trust for himself to make sure that his house couldn't be taken from him if his production company went under. She helped him create an LLC to protect cash assets.

At 43, Liz did not receive sexual attention from Chance Baris, which she was grateful for. She despised him, wildly, but correctly, assuming that he was one of the Hollywood dirtbags who preyed on young women.

And she had spent many a drunken hour with her friend Misty. They've ordered late night food, sat in Liz's hot tub and flirted endlessly. While all of this has happened, Liz signed a lot of documents, even though she didn't remember it.

So when the police approach her about the documents that she signed and notarized, granting Misty everything Chance owned, she acknowledged that they were legit. After all, Chance was dead and he didn't have any living relatives to contest his will. So, Liz thinks, fuck him and the government he rode in on. Maybe she will get some physical attention from Misty now that she has helped her get rich.

-

Detective Mila did not like the fact that Chance had a living trust in place where he left everything to, while cute, Fresno-white-trashy Misty McCarthy. In the week that followed, not a single person confirmed that they were a couple. No one could place them together in a single place besides the club or a random party and not one of those encounters seemed to be romantic. But stranger things have happened.

Still, she thought, she might continue to follow up on McCarthy and Baris. A piece-of-shit silenced pistol with no silencer or numbers. Who can get something like that? Fucking LA people.

She thinks the alcoholic entertainment lawyer who says she remembers Baris signing the documents seems to be lying or hiding something.

But hell, she probably doesn't remember her own middle name at this point in her existence. Elizabeth Crawley had copies of the documents in her own filing cabinet at home, which made it seem more legit, but she also seemed to be surprised to see them there.

How would McCarthy get Baris's safe open to switch the documents? Sleep with him, which is what she did. Maybe it wasn't that complicated.

She found out there was a complaint filed against Baris by someone named Cherice Growler, which was dropped. When she looked into callouts to his address, she found that the police had been called on him seventeen times in the last three years. Some by women, some by men. Dads and boyfriends, she assumes.

Okay so he was a dirtbag. She can't imagine how many actresses he harassed over the years that didn't complain.

Between the drugs, Misty McCallister, James Willis and the probable long history of sexual assault that Baris may have had, there were a lot of people that wouldn't have been sad to see Chance Baris leave this world.

22.

With all that had happened, Lauren didn't have the opportunity to tell James her news. The police were there for hours and they were exhausted by the time they left. They went to the Hermosa house and slept, the detail following them.

The next morning, Lauren tells James that she's moving up north for a while to take care of her mom, Tori, who has cancer. Since it is operable, she thinks it will be for a few months and tells James that she wants the future with him that they had started planning last night.

James completely understands this and tells her that he wishes that he could have spent more time with his parents when they were alive. He can't go with her, needing to be here to run his business, but offers to come up and visit frequently.

With the detail in tow, James drops Lauren off at her apartment a few hours later with most of her stuff.

James and Lauren plan to have dinner the following night. They are both sad about her going up north and neither are looking forward to eating but they do want to spend time together.

When he leaves, Lauren gets a call from Detective Mila, who asks some pretty obvious questions.

Detective Mila: 'Just to confirm, James picked you up from the airport today and you were with him all day?'

Lauren's phone buzzed with an incoming text but she ignored it: 'Yes. We were hanging out at the house. We ordered food and talked.'

Mila: 'Huh. The detail was there the whole time?

Lauren's phone buzzed again, this time a phone call. She pulled the phone from her ear for a second and saw it was Molly. She declined it.

Lauren: 'I didn't see them, like, all the time, but they were there.'

Mila: 'Did you know that Chance Baris and Christopher Scott were dead?'

Lauren, shocked: 'What? No. When? Just now?'

On occasion, Detective Mila used shock to illicit a reaction. If she knew they were dead, she might know more about it than she was letting on. People slipped up and said incriminating things about how the dead got that way. Guilty people made excuses or justified their actions. Accomplices shared information.

Since she already confirmed their stories with Kenneth's people, she really didn't think Lauren or James had anything to do with it. She needed something more and was doing some fishing.

Mila: 'It seems like last night.'

Lauren: 'Oh no. I guess sometime after Chance shot at us then.' Although Lauren obviously didn't care for these two people very much, she still felt bad that they died prematurely. She asked, 'What about their families?'

Mila: 'We're looking into them now.'

-

Back at the Hermosa house, James texts Misty to tell her that Chance shot up his project house. She replies, 'WHAT?!', then 'I guess that was yesterday because he's dead.'

James calls her and says, 'What?!'

'Yeah,' she says, 'the cops were here asking questions so I asked what this was about and she said Chance and Billy were killed last night. I didn't tell her anything about you so in case, you know...'

James was waiting and realized that she was implying 'in case you killed them'.

'Oh, no. I was with the cops until 1am. Last night Chance shows up at my project house in the Santa Monica, walks in the front door and starts shooting. The security guys came running but he took off.'

Misty says, 'Ohmygod, did anyone get hurt?'

James: 'Thankfully he didn't know how to shoot because the only thing that was hit were some floor-to-ceiling windows.

Misty: 'I didn't think you had anything to do with it. You're a great guy. But, you know, I didn't think the cops should know about us because it would look bad and, maybe, in case you did have something to do with it.'

James thought about that a second. He thought Misty had some toughness to her but didn't think she was capable of something like murder. The fact that she thought he might have had something to do with it confirmed to him that she, most likely, didn't.

Neither mentioned Lauren. It was as if mentioning her name would break the spell and forcing them into reality.

James: 'I don't know how he got this address or how he knew I'd be here but the whole thing was captured on the security cameras.'

Misty: 'Oh so the cops don't think you did it. Good.' She smiled on the last word and he could hear it through the phone.

James: 'Do you know what happened to them?'

Misty: 'No. They didn't tell me. I guess I'll have to look for it on the news.'

-

On Wednesday morning, with most of her stuff in storage, Lauren drives her Kia up the 101 north to Carmel, leaving James alone.

A few days later, James texts Misty to see how she's doing.

-

Misty gets a call Tuesday for a meeting on Friday morning to meet with the lawyers. There are 3. One for the production company, one for the estate (house, club, etc.) and one for the studio that he worked with on Wild. They are sympathetic but abrupt, like engineers, but about law. Like they don't deal with people very often.

Which is good, because they are not able to, or care to, read her feelings on the subject of Chance Baris. In fact, the pretty woman representing the estate seems to be enjoying the fact that he is dead and giving his estate to another woman. Maybe she has had to defend some of his more rapey accusations or has made him keep his hands to himself.

Th estimated value of the assets is in the neighborhood of $40 million. The house is around $6m, club around $4m, residuals from Wild and others around $10m and the production company around $20m, without Chance.

She thought of her brother. She'd pinged Jake's cell again but didn't get a response. She normally got a text back within a few minutes but lately the replies were slower and slower. She now had the resources to help. Was it too late? Was he dead?

She let herself roll back in time to when she was fifteen...

-

She had spent a decent Saturday with her dad at the movies and then grabbing dinner. He seemed clean today, which was good, but said he had plans for later that night, which was bad. When he dropped her off at her mom's (as she'd come to think of it), the night had fully set in and the house was dark. No one home.

The house was in a tract of similar looking houses, all two-story, all with the same square footage and same size yard. Some were painted tan, some were painted terra cotta red, some were painted dark brown, some with slightly reversed layouts. There were three different styles of front doors with glass to choose from originally but some have been changed out for solid wood or adding steel security doors. Their neighborhood was still okay. So many areas of Fresno had gotten bad with the meth problem they had in Fresno. Like the other houses though, Mom's house was showing some wear now, with faded paint and cracks in the stucco.

She let herself in and turned on the lights in the downstairs living room. She thought that something seemed off but she probably just had the jitters, coming home to an empty house on a dark street. She couldn't wait for the clocks to change so it would be lighter out later.

She plopped onto the couch and looked at her phone for an hour or so before heading upstairs to take a shower. On the stairs, she noticed that the sliding back door looked like it was open so she went to it to check. It was closed but not locked, which happened sometimes. Jake would leave it open in case he forgot his keys.

Despite the presumed innocence of it, she flipped the latch to lock the slider but thought that her brother may need to get in and flipped it open again, then pulled a medium-sized knife out of the knife rack on her way past, thinking, 'No one is here to make fun of me for taking the knife.' Upstairs, she took her pajamas, which consisted of gray sweatpants cut into shorts, a comfy soft t-shirt and the knife, with her to the bathroom to shower and locked the door.

After an uneventful shower, she hung up her towel, picked up her knife and phone from the sink and headed to her room. Paranoid, she thought, like an old lady. She was thinking about security doors in her neighborhood and how ridiculous she was being when she stepped out of the bathroom and saw the man in the hallway close to her and getting closer. She jumped, so startled that she almost fell on the floor and dropped the knife. For a brief moment, she realized how people can be overcome by panic.

That's Randy, she thought, recognizing him. The recognition gave her comfort for a second, thinking it's okay because she knows him. But then she remembered that Randy was not okay at all. He dated her mom once or twice, meeting Misty once, asking a lot of questions. She thought he seemed nice, that he was interested in kids, like maybe he had some, but mom broke it off with him quickly, never saying what happened between them but making a comment like 'bad call' or something. She couldn't remember.

But here he was in her hallway walking toward her in black jeans and a ratty black tee. He smelled bad, like chemical bad and she didn't know what caused it but thought maybe meth.

She was shying away from him, him on her left side, and remembered the knife in her right hand. She turned toward him and swung the knife at his midsection, cutting his shirt a little and his stomach a lot. The shirt moved with the swing but the tip of the blade still cut him.

He paused as he was about to grab her, realizing something had happened, but maybe the pain hadn't registered yet. He looked down to check where she swung the knife and covered his midsection with his left hand. Blood lightly seeping through his fingers and onto his shirt.

Calm now, momentary panic gone, she brought the knife up to next to her right ear and stuck it into Randy's right shoulder, between his trapezius and his collar bone, pulling it right back out quickly. She did not want to leave her only weapon in his shoulder.

He groaned and tried to swat at her with his right hand, missing entirely as she backed up. Panic seemed to grab him then, his eyes going wide, and he turned, ran down the stairs and out through the sliding door.

Misty didn't know what to do so she called her mom first, thinking she needed Randy's last name to give to the police. She thought about adding some panic into her voice so that her mom doesn't think she's a total sociopath and decided to talk fast instead. Her mom picked up on the second ring, knowing that if her tween daughter is calling on the phone instead of texting, something must be wrong. Mom said she was on her way and calling the police, that Misty should lock the doors and lock herself in her room.

But Misty didn't. She went downstairs and found the back slider standing open, left that way by a fleeing, bleeding Randy. She locked it. She thought that she should get another knife, a bigger one, and even though she was a little shaken, she was not scared. She'd get him in the neck next time, if she had the chance. She thought, if she had to, she could have hurt him very badly and gotten away with it, being all of five feet two inches to Randy's six feet plus, and possibly half his weight.

The thought didn't excite her but didn't repulse her either. She definitely didn't like the sound of the knife going into or coming out of Randy's shoulder but would do it again. She calmly made a mental note to start a gym membership.

Mom and the police arrived, with a lot of worry from mom and questions from the police. They didn't take evidence or dust for fingerprints or any of those cop show things.

Even after that, mom wasn't around very much. She thought, in the wake of the stabbing, she would at least see more of her for a week or so but no. She was home alone most times.

23.

Detective Mila called someone she knew in Narcotics to see Scott or Baris were known in their circles.

Detective Charlie Nelson was an old friend that she knew from her earlier years in uniform. He tried to recruit her into his unit, knowing having another bilingual investigator on the team would help but she declined. Drugs were not her thing and she knew people would know it too.

When Mila asked about them, Charlie replied, 'The *actors*?', which ruled out the probability of the drug angle for her.

So, who else had motive and access? Misty McCarthy. But everyone, including her, had an alibi.

She was stumped, but would keep tabs on McCarthy...

There were a few things Misty didn't like about doing this with Chance and Billy. She didn't like the blood and gore but thought that she would never have to do it again. Hopefully.

Most of all, she didn't like sleeping with Chance. Mercifully she only had to do it twice to get his passwords and open his safe. She upped the dosage on the sleeping medication she stole from Liz's house the third time and it put him out faster, sparing her from that experience again.

She drugged Billy on their first meeting at his house, stole his house keys and went back when he was passed out. She found a spare key and took that, returning his regular set of house keys to their place by the front door.

The timing of the events was where the genius was. She was proud of the intelligence-gathering, the well-placed text messages, the driving between places, leaving her phone at the bar in a drawer, dumping the burner. She thought about how clever the whole thing was, but she would never tell anyone.

The fact that her fellow bartender, Mikey, was drunk most of the time helped. He had no idea how long she went to dinner for. She could be gone twenty minutes or two hours, he didn't notice.

So it was easy to follow James to Santa Monica and get the address. It was easy to leave for 2 hours to shoot Chance, text Billy and let herself into Billy's house and drug his drink before he got back.

The cops may or may not check Billy for sleeping medication but may not think anything of it. It wasn't a lethal dose or anything.

Sooner or later the cops will find a hair of hers in with the dryer lint. Misty was surprised they hadn't already.

She thought, you shouldn't always trust your bartender. Everyone trusted the bartender to make them drinks, and several people let her make them drinks in their homes.

Misty didn't think that password keepers that can be opened by thumbprint were safe at all.

Most of all, Misty thought, if you are willing to do unpleasant things, you can get anything you want in life.

And right now, she wants James. She picked up her phone to text him back.

Epilogue

The Fluffernauts gets picked up by Nickelodeon and a Creative Director (the adopted child of a Hollywood power couple) is added, probably just to attach a name to it, David Whitehall thinks. A typical Hollywood advertising move. Dave, and most of his ideas about the characters, are sidelined for this brat, but they paid him and he retained some of his rights. Could have been worse.

The 'brat' turns out to be a genius and makes the alien muppets into a show, stuffed characters and an app that is free to download but has in-app purchases. The stuffies catch fire first, right before Christmas, and launches the Fluffernauts (all jokes aside) into the billion-dollar franchise world. David is seen as an eccentric, brilliant creative type, which is not exactly correct, but he isn't in the business of correcting people.

-

Tony Saldino comes from a small town near the border between France and Italy, on the coast. Tony's family owns land in the area, and a lot of it. Most was acquired several hundred years ago by the first monarch of Monaco, Honoré II, and more purchased since, the family holding onto it even when the region was taken over by the French. The family estate has property in Nice, Cannes, Monaco and most of Cape Martin in France and Bordighera in Italy.

Since they went to Cannes every year, his grandparents sent him to California to 'look into' the movie business more. In reality, they just wanted him away from the family estate to have some fun and maybe learn a little about the world. He would stay anonymous since the family didn't want some gold-digging actress to make their way into their family. Look at what happened to Johnny Depp, after all.

Also, Tony was not the sharpest knife in the drawer. With him hidden away, they can groom his younger brother to take over the estate one day.

He took the bouncer job to get close to Chance and maybe into some movies. When Tony agreed to go with Billy to help out Chance, he thought it was more of a game that Chance and Lauren played. He didn't get the game at all but people here were weird and kinky, which he thought could be fun.

He woke up in the hospital with broken ribs, which hurt like hell, and a concussion. He doesn't know how he got to the hospital or what day it was but he didn't want to stay.

The hospital administrator came in for payment and he paid with his black Amex. When the nurse came back, he told her he was leaving. The doctor came and prescribed some medicines that he probably wouldn't take and okayed him to leave.

He decided that LA people weren't weird and kinky but completely fucked up. Tony wanted to go back to his villa and drive his Ferrari around the coast for a while.

But he couldn't go home yet. His family wanted him to 'see the world' and only one year wouldn't be enough for them. When the cab dropped him at his rental house in the Holmby Hills, he packed some clothes and took his car to the airport. He was in desperate need of a vacation and had been planning to take a month or two exploring Hawaii.

Which he did.

Author's Notes

This book is a work of fiction. Everything and everyone in it are made up, except the places that aren't.

I've always enjoyed reading stories that have actual places in them. A place you can look up on Google Maps. It sort of allows me to connect the fiction to reality. To relay that through to you, there are a few places that are real, like El Texate on Pico and Sharkee's on the pier in Hermosa. There is no Blue Katana in Hollywood but there was a Red Buddha. The Playboy Diner is modeled after Swingers in Santa Monica that is now closed.

-

Anyone who has seen an athlete jump from the foul line, float down court and slam a basketball might know that we weren't capable of that fifty years ago. The speed at which cars travel on average has doubled in my lifetime. We are physically evolving at an amazing rate and learning more about our brains all the time, despite the occasional interjection in our lives by some of our worst humans trying to push us backward to whatever they're comfortable with, like racism.

The science behind how fast the human race is evolving over the last 100 years is fascinating to me, and what I wrote about it here (which isn't much, scientifically speaking) was researched for accuracy.

Hopefully you enjoy reading it as much as I enjoyed writing it, even though I feel like it is not my story. It's more like this story was somewhere already but I needed to find it, translate it and edit it 200 times.

More to come...

- Pete

www.ingramcontent.com/pod-product-compliance
Lightning Source LLC
Chambersburg PA
CBHW010142030826
48979CB00028B/2164/J
9798991241762